CLOUDS IN THE ATTIC

written by
Todd Alan Dale

CLOUDS IN THE ATTIC

Copyright - February 20, 1988

First Published - August 1995

All Scripture references are taken from the New King James Bible

CLOUDS IN THE ATTIC

...is for the glory and to honor the Blessed Trinity: God the Father, God the Son, and God the Holy Spirit, Who if not for Their reality this story would only be fantasy.

...has been written for Christopher's twelve friends, those individuals named in chapters 2 & 29, who in reality are the friends I cherished while living in South Lake Tahoe, Nevada, during the years 1973-1977. My prayer is that each of the twelve embrace God's gift of everlasting life that was purchased with the blood of Jesus Christ.

...is in memory of my dear friend, Donny Standridge, who has gone on before me to Heaven. On the glorious Day of Resurrection I will behold him anew and together we will enter into the presence of the precious Lamb of God.

...is dedicated to my wife Jennifer and our daughters Rachel, Rebekah, Hannah, and Sarah as well as my parents, family, and friends whose prayers and words of encouragement over the years have enabled me to persevere and complete this long-awaited manuscript.

...was inspired by C.S. Lewis whose wonderful tales fascinated me as a child, all leading to faith in the Aslan of the Bible. Lastly, I must thank Phil Keaggy and Kerry Livgren both of whom have inspired me to paint with words and yearn for Heaven. *What a Day* it will be *When Things Get Electric* and we *Rejoice* while *Racing Away* to those *Golden Halls*, praising *The High and Exalted One* for His grace and mercy.

Chapter Titles

1
The Attic

"The wind blows where it wishes, and you hear the sound of it, but cannot tell where it comes from and where it goes. So is everyone who is born of the Spirit."
John 3:8

Sailing beneath the starry host that summer night the Holy Breeze was cool and refreshing but with Him there came a sense of urgency. The moon watched between fervent marching clouds as the Breeze descended and flowed down a peaceful street, His unexpected arrival being announced cheerfully by the trees whose leaves rustled with delight.

Coming into view was the familiar two-story brick house whereby ivy climbed the edifice's left side, grasping onto a balcony above. It was there glass-paned doors clothed with curtains of white silk swung outward, beckoning the Breeze to enter the attic. Prior engagements at the residence had been cause for celebration but this appointment was of grave importance and so without hesitation He eagerly proceeded between the doors, dancing with their curtains along the way.

Items commonly found in a loft lay scattered about. There was an antique sewing machine, a cherrywood hope chest, two old-fashioned bicycles overcome with rust, and boxes of clothing whose styles had not been seen in decades. Albums of black and white photographs recalling a simpler day and age were stacked unevenly upon the floor. Although dust covered the beloved keepsakes like a winter's snow the attic was warm with memories.

The nostalgia, however, did not concern the Breeze. Indeed, the purpose of His visit was before Him: laying in a bed dressed in blue and white striped pajamas, top buttoned crookedly, was a boy whose cheeks were stained with tiny drops of sorrow. Abounding with compassion the Breeze combed through the youth's hair, caressed his small frame with unconditional love, and then swept out of the attic, satisfied knowing His mission of bringing peace to the boy would soon be fulfilled.

The night was again calm and the old brick house slept soundly. Without warning, a grandfather clock downstairs began chiming and the air tingled with anticipation. Anyone present in the attic that night would have sensed something incredible was about to occur, anyone that is but Christopher.

2
Sorrow at Sunset

A merry heart makes a cheerful countenance,
but by sorrow of the heart the spirit is broken.
Proverbs 15:13

In all honesty Christopher had noticed very little all day. As he and his family traveled that afternoon from the majestic mountains to a city in the valley his mind had been numb, his ears deaf, and his eyes indifferent to all that had passed before them. He was apathetic towards everyone and upon arriving at his grandparents' only welcomed their hugs halfheartedly; his behavior, quite frankly, bordered on rudeness. During supper Christopher had asked to be excused on account of a stomachache and upon receiving approval from concerned faces around the table wished everyone a 'goodnight' and retreated to his temporary bedroom in the attic.

Before reaching the top stair his eyes had overflowed with tears. Without bothering to turn on the light he closed the door, stumbled to his suitcase, shed his clothes and shoes, carelessly threw on his blue and white striped pajamas, and collapsed on the bed.   He remained undisturbed in his troubled thoughts until an embrace and prayer from his mother at nightfall divided the long day from the eternal night.

His sorrow had really begun a few months earlier when due to financial reasons it was necessary his family relocate.   This was sad news to them all but for Christopher, being just ten years of age, it was especially devastating knowing he would be separated from many dear friends.   Lying back on the bed his twelve classmates convincingly roamed the ceiling above: there were Scott and Kevin, Christopher's closest and best friends; Stephen, the greatest handball player ever; Karen and Dave, the two who consistently earned straight A's in school; Julie, whose kind heart was always appreciated; Andy and David, the class pranksters whose jokes could cheer up anyone; Barbie, who knew a little about everything; Buddy and Jeff, who were best of friends themselves; and last of all was Natalie who Christopher believed was the most beautiful girl in the whole world.

Moonlight peeked intermittently through the clouds, kissing the boy's tear-streaked face. He was overwhelmed with despair knowing though only a hundred miles distanced himself from his friends, they were now in the most forsaken way worlds apart. In the weeks and months to come Christopher could only wonder what interests preoccupied their lives as they continued sharing life together without him. Worst of all, in only a few short years their remembrance of him would fade leaving only bittersweet memories and this broke his heart.

With the grandfather clock striking nine o'clock a dense carpet of mist streamed into the attic and billowed around the bed, abruptly interrupting his misery. A foaming tide then arose, brushing the ceiling above and swallowing him in a sea of white. Gasping in disbelief Christopher sat up to discover peering down at him was a man made entirely of clouds!

3
A Heavenly Visitor

Blessed be the God and Father of our Lord Jesus Christ
the Father of mercies and God of all comfort...
2 Corinthians 1:3

Christopher was speechless. Amazed and uncertain as to what had entered into his grandparents' attic he stared in awe up at the inexplicable creature whose swirling mass hovered before him. The being's lower body, rooted in the blanketing fog, resembled a large tree trunk. From the waist up a husky torso supported enormous shoulders whereby brawny arms, spread out like branches, sustained powerful hands. The immense size of the creature's frame was a deceiving compliment to its head that was crowned with long white hair. Nestled beneath its stern nose grew a mustache and feathery beard, both of which flowed around a congenial mouth. The facial characteristic most mesmerizing were its beautiful tranquil eyes, both of which mirrored great sympathy that Christopher realized was for himself.

"Do not feel ashamed," spoke a deep and gentle voice. "It is the shedding of tears that heals a broken spirit."

"Thank you, sir," Christopher began awkwardly, drying his blushing cheeks.

"I am pleased to see you are not afraid of me, Christopher," the being smiled warmly.

Surprisingly, Christopher felt no fear. The questions bursting in his head did not provide him enough time to worry whether the creature was friendly or not. What was *it* that stood over him? Why was *it* here? More importantly, how did *it* know his name?

"My name is Cumulus," the heavenly visitor began humbly, "and as a servant of the Creator, I, along with others like myself encompass your world and nourish it daily with rain."

"Are you a *'Cloud Man'*?" Christopher asked in amazement.

"You see me for who I am," Cumulus affirmed cheerfully.

"I have always dreamed of walking on fluffy clouds," Christopher sighed, momentarily forgetting his sorrow.

"The fulfillment of those dreams is at hand for I have been appointed by the Creator, His Son, and the Holy Breeze to bear you above, answering the faithful prayers of your family."

"Perhaps I am going to be reunited with my friends!" The boy uttered excitedly.

"Or perhaps," the Cloud Man added tenderly, "the Creator will glorify Himself by bestowing you contentment through heartache."

4
March of the Clouds

Who covers the heavens with clouds, Who prepares rain for the earth,
Who makes grass to grow on the mountains.
Psalm 147:8

Preoccupied with buttoning his pajama top properly Christopher did not hear the Cloud Man's response. Rummaging through disheveled clothing within his suitcase, he located a red sweatshirt, pulled it over his head, quickly stepped out of the pajama bottoms, and wiggled into a pair of blue jeans.

"Your eagerness is a welcomed sight," Cumulus stated joyfully, "for I am in a bit of a hurry. Rain is expected in the east late tonight and the march has already begun."

"Will I get wet?" Christopher asked over his shoulder, searching in his suitcase for a clean pair of socks. "Should I bring a raincoat?"

"That will not be necessary," Cumulus chuckled, "for you will remain dry."

Christopher hurriedly pulled on the socks and slipped into his tennis shoes. While tying the laces he paused and looked up anxiously at Cumulus. "Will I be home before dawn?"

"You need not worry," the Cloud Man said reassuringly, "for the Master of Time Himself will ensure your timely return."

Christopher sighed with relief, finished dressing, and replied, "I am ready now."

"Before we embark on the journey," Cumulus spoke soberly, "I must forewarn you that releasing your hold of my hand while in the sky would not be safe."

Christopher nodded in understanding. Cumulus extended his large hand down to him but the boy hesitated, looking out between the balcony's doors and into the night beyond.

"It may do your faith some good knowing you are not the first human to travel by cloud," Cumulus commented with a grin.

Accepting those words as a pledge, Christopher reached up and found his hand instantly enveloped by the soft but firm grip of the

Cloud Man. With a gentle pull and a great rush of air he discovered himself floating above the floor, body being ushered between the glass-paned doors. Hair being blown about the face, Christopher and his newfound friend of white pilgrimaged upwards leaving behind the attic and its sorrows.

Below, the city's lights sparkled like diamonds but his attention was quickly drawn heavenward where an enormous assembly of clouds came into sight. Nearing the mammoth formation Christopher perceived its expanse constituted thousands of personages similar to Cumulus, some appearing as men while others resembling women but despite their gender all beamed gestures of welcome his way. Joining their assemblage, the corporate gathering of benevolent creatures advanced across the sky, carrying rain to the thirsty earth below.

Christopher next noticed a large valley emerging at a lower elevation in the clouds and it was there two other creatures congregated. The first resembled gray boulders, obese yet boasting small rugged heads. Due to their weight they walked about the plain slowly, creating depressions on the cloud floor with every footstep. The second party of characters maintained the opposite physical characteristics being they were slender, very tall, and possessed shiny white bodies, compelling the boy to squint.

"Who are *they?*" Christopher questioned in bewilderment.

"They, too, are servants of the Creator," Cumulus spoke admiringly. "The gray individuals are appropriately named *'Thunderheads'* and the tall shiny beings are *'Lightnings'*. Watch as they honor the Creator in their service to Him but take my advice and cover your ears!"

Christopher looked on in anticipation as both parties amused him with their comical performances in the sky. The Thunderheads began huddling into clusters of seven and after turning around walked away from their corresponding bunch. Having created a large circle by distancing themselves from one another, they pivoted around and with all their might ran (Christopher thought it was more like waddling) back towards their assigned group. Prior to the unavoidable collisions

Christopher wisely leaned his head against the soft body of Cumulus while using his free hand to cover the other ear. The impact echoed throughout the sky with a reverberating sound.

BOOOOMMMMMMMM!

BOOOOMMMMMMMM!

BOOOOMMMMMMMM!

BOOOOMMMMMMMM!

While the Thunderheads slowly regained their footing Christopher was treated to another fantastic display of elemental activity as the Lightnings began diving headlong through the cloud floor. Stretching to outrageous lengths, their bodies crackled and flashed brightly with a yearning to touch the earth and though few were successful, all were content illuminating the night sky.

It then began to rain. Cumulus had spoken truthfully for the boy did not get wet but rather found himself witnessing a spectacular sight: every cloud person on the plateau began dancing, their forms bobbing and swaying rhythmically to an inaudible song! Obediently holding onto Cumulus' hand Christopher joined the Cloud People by going through the motions yet feeling silly all the while.

"Without our dance," Cumulus explained, "it cannot rain. Our willingness to move joyfully releases the liquid of life from our innermost being, allowing us to water your world."

With those words of encouragement Christopher danced enthusiastically with the Cloud People until the sacrificial promenade concluded.

"We will soon be separating from the march for your destination is nigh," Cumulus spoke with anticipation. "Perhaps before we depart you will have an opportunity to witness the Rainbow People. They are the kindred whom the Creator has assigned the 'Promise'."

Moments later and rising up out from the cloud's floor were thousands of colorfully clothed people, each dressed in the most brilliant blues, greens, yellows, oranges, reds, and purples, hand in hand according to their respective colors.

"The Creator initially granted their show in the heavens following the Great Flood," the Cloud Man reminisced. "They are His covenant to mankind that never again will the earth be covered entirely with water." Bending down to whisper, Cumulus' beard tickled the boy's ear. "I have heard it said that during the Great Flood the Thunderheads were complaining of migraines...but that is only a rumor!" Cumulus roared a hearty laugh.

As the Rainbow People ascended, dazzling all with their arch of colorful splendor, Christopher and his companion of white began their descent, bidding farewell to the great march in the sky.

5
The Fountain of Living Waters

Jesus answered and said to her, "Whoever drinks of this water will thirst again, but whoever drinks of the water that I shall give him will never thirst. But the water that I shall give him will become in him a fountain of water springing up into everlasting life."
John 4:13-14

Sunlight shimmered upon an ocean of blue, green, and purple, its waves bowing with thanksgiving upon a pristine beach of an island. A short distance from the shore arose a broad causeway accessible only by a granite staircase. Climbing the steps with his eyes, Christopher followed from its pinnacle a red graveled pathway, weaving through lush foliage and mature trees, culminating where he glimpsed the summit of an immense and mysterious stone building.

"Welcome to the Island of Time," Cumulus announced merrily. "The moment setting foot on this land you will be instantly refreshed and for the duration of your stay will not experience fatigue, hunger, or thirst. It is a small taste of the new world to come."

After dancing many hours with the Cloud People Christopher was indeed tired and famished but Cumulus proved again trustworthy as the boy was renewed and satisfied once stepping foot on the island.

"Atop the stairs is a path leading to your destination," the Cloud Man smiled. "There you will find, I pray, the contentment of your soul. I have thoroughly enjoyed your company, Christopher. Perhaps I will be privileged to escort you home once your adventure is complete. May your heart find fulfillment by the grace and mercy of the Creator," Cumulus concluded and speedily ascended, leaving wisps of himself behind.

Combing his hair and smoothing out his sweatshirt Christopher walked over to the staircase, took a deep breath, and briskly jogged up the steps. Although steep, he reached the summit full of vigor and so without breaking momentum eagerly strode upon the red gravel, indulging himself with the aromatic flowers and impeccably manicured lawns. Perceiving the sound of running water, he spied ahead and discovered the pathway encircled an elevated pool at whose center a fountain ruptured joyfully. Beyond the pool seven steps progressed upwards to the colossal edifice: cathedral in appearance, the building exulted domes, steeples, and towers while flying buttresses silhouetted the heavens with their magnificent leaps of faith.

Splashing water directed his attention again towards the fountain and though not thirsty, he was irresistibly drawn to drink from its offering. Gazing into the crystal liquid he was startled there was no reflection of himself on its surface. It was then he first heard the Voice, softly but intensifying by the moment, calling out lovingly…

"Oh, taste and see that the LORD is good;

Blessed is the man who trusts in Him!"

Although the Voice was compassionate Christopher's heart fostered pride, enabling both bitterness and sorrow to control his soul. Unable to liberate himself from resentment he walked away from the living water, rejecting the gift and its cleansing power.

19

6
Canvas of Creation

"It is a sign between Me and the children of Israel forever;
for in six days the LORD made the heavens and the earth,
and on the seventh day He rested and was refreshed."
Exodus 31:17

Brooding with scorn, Christopher mounted the building's steps and stood in the shadow of massive oak doors. Reaching up to announce his arrival both doors unexpectedly swung inward yet his friends, nor any host for that matter, were present. Disappointed and frustrated, he nonetheless felt beckoned to enter the enigmatic monument and so not wishing to decline the invitation stepped across the threshold into a spacious narthex, the doors closing silently behind him. Above him light streamed through stained glass windows, splashing vivid hues upon the marble floor while directly ahead, hanging between arched portals to his left and right, was an enormous curtain of crimson velvet at whose right edge was a braided sash. Curious, he approached the cord and gave it a slight tug, persuading the weighty veil to rise, revealing a gold-framed ebony canvas. Reaching out with defiance to touch the behemoth exhibition, Christopher was instead surprised to discover a void of immeasurable depth.

Suddenly, a word in an unintelligible language bellowed forth from within the canvas followed by a tremendous explosion of light. Out of nowhere, out of nothing, *it* was there and despite being at a great distance Christopher watched in fascination as the blue sphere of water rotated slowly upon its axis. Flying towards him from the spinning globe was a girl whose long brown hair lashed about the white gown that clung tenaciously to her slender body. Momentum slowing, she passed through the gilded frame and gently landed barefoot before him, face beaming with uncontrollable joy.

"My name is Sunday," the girl exclaimed happily and stooping, kissed him on the forehead, provoking his cheeks to blush, "the first of the seven Daughters of Time."

"But-," Christopher blurted.

"*Ssshhhh,*" Sunday whispered and stepped to his side, slipping her left hand into his right. "Just watch and enjoy," she said gazing with anticipation into the canvas.

Directing his attention to the living picture Christopher saw the new world was much closer now. The water then divided, creating a vapor awning above while the remaining liquid below consisted as one great ocean below. Another girl, this one dressed in a gown of blue, soared through the frame and stood before him grinning from the inside out.

"My name is Monday," she affirmed, kissed his forehead, and proceeded by taking hold of his left hand. Without needing to be reminded he turned towards the canvas of life.

The ocean receded and dry ground appeared with mountains and valleys forming, all existing as a singular continent. Grass, bushes, trees, and all types of vegetation landscaped the earth with verdant growth. Christopher did not stir from his reverie until again being kissed.

"My name is Tuesday," the girl clothed in green smiled and tenderly reaching for Sunday's right hand.

The ever-changing panorama abruptly shifted, directing Christopher to focus on the outer darkness where spectacular flashes of white, each birthing a star and awakening the young cosmos with light. A great blast of energy then produced a blazing orb of heat followed subsequently by planets, skating around the pulsating sun with cosmic affection.

"I am Wednesday," the girl clothed in yellow stated warmly. She, too, kissed his forehead and quickly occupied the space beside her sister Monday.

A different type of explosion now occurred as the ocean began teeming with fins, gills, and all sorts of aquatic life while the sky filled with a multitude of colorful birds.

Yet another girl stood before Christopher, this one dressed in orange.

"Thursday," he voiced with full assurance.

She smiled, kissed him on the forehead and secured her place next to Tuesday.

There was now movement upon the terrestrial plain as animals of all colors, shapes, and sizes, fur or scales, claws or hooves, and even creatures found only in picture books roamed the land. Christopher then saw *them* in the most beautiful garden: they were young, healthy, and most important content.

"I am Friday," said the girl in red. Like her sisters, she kissed Christopher's forehead and gently took Wednesday's free hand.

The new world was indeed a testimony to the Creator's love: there was no pollution, weeds, pain, tears, or death; everything was peaceful, perfect, and good.

Approaching Christopher and the six Daughters of Time from within the Canvas of Creation was one last girl wearing a gown of royal purple and a smile of victory.

"Christopher, you have just witnessed the Creation," Saturday exclaimed joyfully, "the age between the two eternities."

7
The Library of Time

For God will bring every work into judgment,
including every secret thing, whether good or evil.
Ecclesiastes 12:14

Seven ageless girls beamed with delight at Christopher. He on the other hand returned an expression of uncertainty.

"You need not worry," Saturday spoke reassuringly, "for we are the Daughters of Time and have been brought into existence by the Creator, through His Son, and by the power of the Holy Breeze, all for Their glory."

The boy nodded sheepishly and then peered into the frame. For him the beauty of the new world was so close yet unapproachable.

"Christopher, it is true your First Parents rebelled and cursed the Creator's gift of life," Wednesday began gravely but progressed to hope. "The Creator's Son, however, has since purchased with His own blood everlasting life for those whom the Holy Breeze calls. Once this

25

Age of Sorrows has passed the Creator will glorify His Creation and fellowship in righteousness with the Elect for eternity future."

Ignoring this good news he stared despairingly at the sisters. There was no purpose in living if he could not be with his friends.

"When can I see them?" he blurted aloud.

"See *who*?" the sisters asked, exchanging puzzled glances.

"Well, my friends of course," he replied sassily.

"Perhaps he means *'when will I begin the journey'*," Thursday exclaimed optimistically.

"Oh, yes, the journey," the girls chorused in agreement.

"Yes, the journey to see my-"

"You will be leaving at sunset this very day," Tuesday explained graciously, "but before you leave we must first show you the Library, the Clock, and the Tree. Come, let us go now."

Without an opportunity to explain himself, Sunday and Monday walked Christopher towards the right side of the Creation Canvas where a set of double doors opened on their own accord.

"Christopher," Sunday announced with great emotion, "welcome to the Library of Time."

Escorted through the doorway he discovered the universe did not inhabit the adjacent room but rather a grand hall, permeated with the scent of antiquity, harbored a myriad of books. Occupying the wood shelves seven stories high the majority of tomes bulged with pages though some were so slim they subsist of only a single sheet.

"What stories do these books tell?" his question echoed throughout the athenaeum.

"Each declares the life story of every person who has ever or who ever will live," Monday volunteered. "Sadly, many of these books record the lives of the Exiles," she added grievously.

"Who are the '*Exiles*'?" Christopher asked apprehensively.

Tears welling up in their eyes the sisters halted and faced the youth.

"They are the people," Thursday lamented, "who during this Age of Sorrows rejected the Creator's love and selfishly lived for themselves and by doing so served the Dark Emperor. Their names not being found in the Book of Life they now hopelessly await the Day of Judgment."

Thursday's words gripped Christopher's spirit, body, and soul with fear realizing he likewise was guilty of this offense and efforts to cleanse his conscience were in vain.

Traversing down the center aisle the small party came to a clearing and it was there a shorter corridor intersected from the left and right, signifying the library was in the shape of a cross. At these crossroads was a grand dais of red marble whereupon sat a remarkable instrument: internal mechanisms set in motion a pendulum, employing sable arms to revolve above a pale-faced dial, void of numbers, all for marking the days remaining in this current epoch.

"We await the Creator's Son," Friday beamed triumphantly, "Who will someday ride upon the clouds from Heaven and halt the Clock of Time, banishing forever this Age of Sorrows and establish a kingdom of righteousness."

Although silent the timepiece loudly proclaimed a sobering truth: the Creator demonstrates mercy by patiently waiting for all to humbly repent of pride and yet justice as well in that He will not endure mankind's rebellion forever.

"Christopher," Monday stated his name with emphasis, "the purpose of bringing you to the island lies in what you will be shown next for in it hangs the balance of hope and despair, peace and chaos, life and death for many who await its promise."

8
The Tree of Life

Blessed are those who do His commandments,
that they may have the right to the tree of life...
Revelation 22:14a

It was twilight when Christopher and the Daughters of Time congregated in a courtyard where the air was bathed in the invigorating fragrances of gardenia and honeysuckle.

"Christopher," Tuesday said reverently, "behold, the Creator's wedding gift to His future bride: the Tree of Life."

A pavilion of ribbed columns faithfully upheld an alabaster cupola where beneath, abiding in serenity, was an ivory tree flourishing with emerald leaves. Suspended upon graceful boughs was fruit whose iridescent skin revealed golden nectar, radiating forth everlasting life.

"The Tree was transplanted here after the Fall," Friday voiced somberly. "One day all who have been chosen by the Creator and cleansed by the blood of His Son will eat its fruit and live forever."

30

"But the fruit looks ripe now," he remarked impatiently, failing to comprehend the gift, its great cost, and purpose.

"Yes, Christopher," Thursday responded with assurance, "it is always in season but the hearts' of all who will partake of it are not as of yet. The Creator's affairs are not subject to our schedule."

Convening beneath the dome Sunday pointed to the tree's base.

"Look, Christopher."

He saw reposing upon rich topsoil an object the shape and size of a walnut, its surface sheathed in thorns and glistening with blood.

"This seed has been sacrificially harvested by the Creator's Son," Saturday spoke passionately, "and it has been appointed for you to carry this gift to the people in the Land of the Four Kingdoms who have been awaiting His promise of everlasting life."

"Are you not going with me?" Christopher asked slightly irritated, continuing to disregard the message of forgiveness that was also for himself.

31

"I am sorry, Christopher," Wednesday said sympathetically, "but we are not permitted to leave the Island of Time. Do not be troubled, though many covet the seed for ill purposes there will be those you meet whom the Creator loves and they will care for you."

Friday knelt and retrieved from the inside of her gown a small wood box. Opening the lid, she carefully closed the vessel over the seed, capturing the legacy of love within.

"Are you willing to share the Creator's love with those who are longing for the fulfillment of His promise?" Saturday asked.

Although the moment was solemn Christopher's face broke into a grin: perhaps delivering the seed would earn him a reunion with his friends! Selfishly he nodded, prompting Sunday to latch the coffer and once handing it to him tucked the treasure in his front pocket.

"You must use discretion when sharing knowledge of the seed with others," Monday expressed gravely. "Although it cannot be taken from you by force, it can, however, be given away freely. Take care to guard the motives of your heart."

"Let us now depart from here," Sunday concluded with earnest, "for you have a long journey ahead and it is of utmost urgency you begin right away."

9
Judgment Day

And I saw the dead, small and great, standing before God, and books were opened.
And another book was opened, which is the Book of Life. And the dead were judged
according to their works, by the things which were written in the books.
Revelation 20:12

Descending stairs on the island's eastern side, the Daughters of Time and Christopher walked to the water's edge where Tuesday brought forth a silver whistle and blew upon it sharply. Although no sound was heard there was a sight to be seen: approaching the island at a persistent pace was a gigantic sea turtle, its shell adorned with an enormous basket brimming with velvet pillows.

"Christopher," Friday smiled, "your ride has arrived."

The aquatic creature positioned itself against the shoreline and the boy bravely climbed into its bassinet. No longer associated with the island Christopher succumb to exhaustion, granting the cushions to cradle his weary body. Not to be overlooked, his stomach announced its emptiness with a raucous grumble, inducing the sisters to giggle.

"Rest easy," Thursday smiled, "your voyage is guaranteed to be safe. Once arriving at the Land of the Four Kingdoms you will find a garden with bushes bearing wonderful tasting berries so do not hesitate to eat them. We urge you to then direct your steps toward the East Kingdom where you will present the seed to the king and queen who govern there."

"Thank you," Christopher yawned, his eyelids being uncontrollably drawn shut.

"Farewell seed-bearer," Sunday called out merrily.

The words of the seventh sister were drowned out by the waves that soothed him with a sweet lullaby. Drifting out of consciousness, dark shadows clouded his sight and with familiar shapes materializing, Christopher found himself once again in the Library of Time. As before, the books sat motionless and the clock moved silently.

Without warning a trumpet sounded and the clock abruptly stopped: time had come to an end! The extraordinary timepiece gleamed with light, miraculously transforming into a great white throne with One seated upon it in glorious splendor. Christopher then watched with trepidation as the Holy Breeze roared throughout the cross-shaped theatre, breathing onto every volume, stirring them to life: red, yellow, black and white, young and old, Elect and Exile alike came forth to face the Day of Judgment.

Humanity's tide ebbed and flowed with Christopher being tossed to and fro amongst the masses, some cheering and dancing with unbridled joy though many more wailed and writhed in anguish. Above the swelling clamor a figure bobbed, toiling ever closer and howling words of regret that soon became painfully clear.

"Christopher, why did you not drink from the Fountain of Living Waters when you had the opportunity? Now it is too late!"

Body seized with fear the person clutched him desperately about the knees. Christopher looked down into the tormented face and realized it was his very own!

10
A Meal Worthing Thinking About

The LORD knows the thoughts of man, that they are futile.
Psalm 94:11

Christopher awoke with a jolt! Wrestling out from under the pillows he was relieved to find himself no longer in the library but instead on the shoreline at the dawn of a new day. A hillside abundant with trees was before him and so quickly disembarking from the aquatic gondola ran with vigor up the slope. Panting for air as he reached its crown, there a garden containing bushes laden with delicious looking berries thrived, prompting his stomach to growl.

Walking over to a bush he immediately experienced the unsettling sensation of being watched. Sweeping his gaze across the landscape he recalled Thursday bestowing him permission to eat from the berry bushes and besides, his stomach would not be denied. Convinced he was alone, Christopher examined the luscious food that grew on its limbs: swirling shades of orange and purple adorned the smooth marble-sized fruit, growing abundantly in clusters and saturating the air with an enticing aroma. Without hesitation he picked a berry from the nearest branch and popped it into his mouth. Anticipating its juices to be sweet and refreshing he was disheartened to discover the fruit had no flavor whatsoever. He felt betrayed. What kind of food was this that teased the senses but failed to produce where it mattered most? It was comparable to receiving a beautifully wrapped Christmas package that was empty inside!

"At least a banana tastes like a banana," he uttered with disappointment.

Without any warning his mouth was instantly filled with the best tasting banana imaginable!

"I could sure use some milk to wash this banana down."

To his delight he was swallowing creamy milk. It then occurred to him that whatever food he was thinking of while eating the fruit would instantaneously be present in his mouth, its flavor and texture being exquisite.

"It has been far too long since I have enjoyed Grandma's roast duck dinner," he sighed with pleasure and so plucked a handful of berries, sat down upon a nearby bench, and commenced eating the most savory banquet ever.

"Some mashed potatoes would be nice."

The potatoes were smooth and buttery with just a hint of salt. He progressed to a tossed green salad drenched in ranch dressing, fresh rolls with raspberry jelly, and then contemplated about more duck.

"For once," the boy laughed aloud, "I will not be told to eat those horrible tasting peas-*AAAGGGGHHHHH!*" He violently spit the berry out from his mouth. "I suppose I had best be careful what I think about," he declared indignantly.

Completing the meal with his favorite dessert, blackberry cobbler, he relished every bite though careful to avoid thinking about the crust.

"I sure wish these bushes grew back where I live," he said dreamily, a smile of contentment creeping over his face.

"Well, since they do not," a cheerful voice spoke from behind, "you had best eat your fill now."

Startled by the verbal intrusion Christopher turned to locate the responsible party. The sun having just risen above the horizon its light revealed a garden boasting a variety of flowers, trees, a small dwelling...and a statue whose face was breaking into a smile!

Christopher marveled for before him animated with life was a man from smooth green stone. Clothed in a white tunic and brown sandals, the living statue toted over his shoulder a canvas satchel abounding with red roses.

"I realize it is early in the morning but I do not look that bad, do I?" questioned the man of stone, his expression growing more cheerful by the moment.

"Who are you?" Christopher asked in disbelief.

"Well, I am the gardener, of course, and a most excellent one at that," the statue answered, extending his hands. "For you see, thorns cannot hurt me," he chuckled with amusement.

40

"Why did you not make your presence known to me?" the boy inquired, both embarrassed and perturbed.

"I watched you enter the garden and begin your meal from the Bushes of Wishful Thinking but you failed to notice me because your stomach was hungrier than your eyes are big," he bellowed forth another jolly laugh.

Christopher rolled his eyes and shook his head.

"Although I neither eat nor drink, I nearly 'cracked-up' after your comment about the peas.   I have heard they are terrible!" and with that last remark the man of stone doubled over in laughter. Christopher could see though the man was physically heavy he was unquestionably light in spirit.

"The last task I remember accomplishing yesterday was pruning this rose bush," the living statue continued.   "I often get carried away with my work and sometimes forget to cease from my duties before sunset."

"What do you mean?" Christopher pressed, totally confused.

41

"Well, if it were not for sun's light continually touching some part of my body I would not have life," he responded appreciatively. "Perhaps it is a reminder of my *fallen* nature," he answered while questioning himself.

"What does sunlight have to do with you being alive? Christopher countered with frustration. "You are not making sense."

"Silly me! Where are my manners? Please, allow me tell you my story," and with those words the man of stone seated himself beside Christopher and began to narrate his very unusual tale.

11
A Testimony Set in Stone

But He answered and said to them,
"I tell you that if these should keep silent, the stones would immediately cry out."
Luke 19:40

"What I am about to tell you happened just before my coming into existence," the statue began mysteriously. "Oh, and by the way, my name is Petra and you will soon know why."

Christopher nodded politely and cast his full attention upon the man of stone.

"This garden belongs to a man by the name of Samuel, bless his soul," Petra began earnestly. "Now Samuel is an elderly and lonely man, having no wife or children. What he did have was an overwhelming amount of gardening chores which were very burdensome. Not long ago, Samuel bitterly cursed the Creator,

"If You truly cared for mortals such as myself You would help me in my old age!"

"Looking out from his bedroom window that night Samuel witnessed a green meteorite plummet from the heavens and land over there," Petra spoke, pointing to a large hole in the ground, "but this angered him all the more when realizing how much time and effort it would take to restore this garden. He would soon learn, however, the disaster was a blessing in disguise...me!" Petra grinned.

"Later that night the Creator's Son entered the garden and with great care began to sculpt me from the stone. The moment my eyes were opened I was blinded by beauty and glory. He was clothed in a robe down to the feet and girded about the chest with a golden belt. His hair was white and His eyes were like flames of fire. His feet were the color of fine brass, as if refined in a furnace, and His hands had been pierced, stained with His own blood. Once my ears could hear He spoke, a Voice resonating like a fountain of living water."

"I am the Creator's Son, the Master Sculptor, and I will see that your completed form honors Me. You will be called 'Petra' for I have made you from stone. As a reminder to Who created you the sunlight alone will give you life."

44

"Throughout the night He labored, shaping me to His perfect will. He finished polishing my body as the sun broke over the mountains in the east and I immediately fell to my knees, worshipping Him in adoration."

"I will serve You all the days of my life," I humbly proclaimed.

"Render service to Me by caring for My chosen servant, Samuel," He commanded joyously…and then vanished!"

Christopher's mouth gaped in astonishment.

"After gazing upon me the following morning, Samuel was to say the least, utterly flabbergasted," Petra continued, "and it took him some time before finally accepting the fact that not only was I alive but also his earthly servant, a gift from the Creator. I faithfully served him and we were closer than brothers but now that he is gone my stone heart aches with his absence."

"What happened to him?" Christopher asked anxiously.

"I do not know," Petra frowned with uncertainty. "A few weeks ago Samuel came to me saying he was leaving on a journey and promised to return shortly. Knowing that at his age traveling alone was not a good idea I offered to accompany him but he stubbornly refused, adamant I remain here and tend the garden. I have not seen nor heard from him since and fear the worst. I have often thought of searching for him but my leaving here would be to disobey his command."

Returning to a more chipper tone, Petra asked, "Now that I have talked your ears off, who are you and where are you going?"

Believing the carefree man of stone could be trusted Christopher narrated his story beginning with his grandparents' attic, proceeded to his journey in the clouds with Cumulus, and concluded with all that had transpired with the Daughters of Time including the Tree of Life and its seed he carried. Due to shame, however, he did not mention his nightmare of Judgment Day.

"I would just 'crumble' to see the authentic Tree of Life," Petra stated longingly. "What a blessing it would be to view the only tree this side of Heaven whose leaves never fade and fruit never spoils."

Not particularly interested in discussing gardening and more particularly anything regarding a sacred nature, Christopher replied, "I do not wish to be rude but I must be on my way and deliver the seed if I am ever again to see my friends."

"I agree wholeheartedly," Petra approved, perceiving Christopher did not yet fully understand the significance of the gift he carried. "Wait here one moment," the man of stone added and quickly ran to Samuel's house. Upon returning his canvas bag now bulged with food and in his hand was a rolled parchment.

"I have packed refreshments and other necessities. This will also be of great assistance," he affirmed unrolling the map, "since neither of us have before traveled in the Land of the Four Kingdoms."

"Will you be going with me?" Christopher asked with surprise. "Are you not to care for Samuel's garden until he returns?"

"After some consideration," Petra mused, "your mission for the Creator is of supreme importance and it is no coincidence you entered this garden. Besides, this is confirmation I go search for Samuel."

12
Journey to the East

The way of the just is uprightness;
O Most Upright, You weigh the path of the just.
Isaiah 26:7

"According to this map," Petra began merrily, "by heading south we will come to a road running from the Great Sea here in the West Kingdom to our desired destination, the palace of the king and queen in the East Kingdom."

They set off at a brisk pace and it was not long when the road Petra mentioned came into view and so turning, traveled eastward toward mountains of grandeur.

"Those are the Hopeful Mountains and they run north to south, dividing the West Kingdom from the East Kingdom," Petra boasted, examining the map. "When we reach their base the road will bend south." His calculations proved correct once again and within the hour they were heading south with the mountains on their left.

While on the road they passed through many villages whereby the man of stone received gazes of wonderment but none of the perplexed faces belonged to his beloved Samuel.

"I am certain," Petra said confidently, "the Creator will care for him until we are together again."

"Your master must indeed be a great friend," Christopher remarked compassionately, "for I, too, know what it is like to be separated from those who are dear to the heart."

Throughout the day Christopher drank water from a flask and snacked on the food Petra had thoughtfully packed: bread, cheese, vegetables, nuts, smoked fish, and berries from the Bushes of Wishful Thinking.

"Those nutritious foods are so I can be certain you are eating well," Petra remarked shrewdly.

Prior to sunset the travelers departed the road and entered a field of haystacks where Petra went *'lifeless'* and Christopher slept peacefully throughout the night at his feet in a bed of yellow straw.

The next morning Christopher busily plucked hay from his hair as Petra made a decision they would soon not forget.

"The Hopeful Mountains on our left will soon give way to a stretch of woodland called the Lost Forest. Journeying another two days south from there will bring us to a pass through the mountains called Traveler's Gap which after another day or so will take us to the East Kingdom. I suggest we spare ourselves a half week of unnecessary walking by taking a shortcut through the Lost Forest."

"Do you think that is a good idea?" Christopher questioned with wrinkled brow. "The name *'Lost Forest'* does not sound reassuring."

"Do not be silly!" Petra spoke presumptuously. "I have a map and we will be traveling eastward. Besides, I am too *'hard-headed'* to say no."

13
Lost in the Forest

I will bring the blind by a way they do not know; I will lead them in paths they have not known. I will make darkness light before them, and crooked places straight. These things I will do for them, and not forsake them.
Isaiah 42:16

After breakfast the travelers arrived at the lower section of the Hopeful Mountain's northern range where to their left a serene woodland of evergreen trees thrived.   Stepping boldly into the foreboding forest Petra maneuvered carefully amongst the trees, mindful of the dense foliage obstructing the sun's rays.   Christopher on the other hand followed less enthusiastically.

As the hours wore on it became apparent one of two things had occurred: either the forest was wider than thought or they were hopelessly lost.   It was late afternoon when both knew the latter was true and no one's heart was heavier than he whose was made of stone.

"Forgive me, it is all my fault!" Petra bemoaned.   "If I had not been so pridefully arrogant we would still be safe and sound on the road. Rather than saving us time I have ended up spending more of it!"

"Well, there is nothing we can do about it now," Christopher sighed, ignoring Petra's confession. "All I care about," pausing as his stomach thundered, "is getting something to eat. I have not had a bite to eat since breakfast and I am starving."

The youth sat down upon a log and began foraging through the knapsack. Petra on the other hand unrolled the map and shook his head.

"I am certain we have been traveling due east. This forest is undoubtedly enchanted," he laughed with frustration.

"What is that over there?" Christopher questioned, taking a bite from a wedge of cheese.

"The East Kingdom," Petra responded smugly, the map engaging his attention.

"No, Petra, over *there*," the boy repeated, pointing over his new-found friend's shoulder.

In the distance was a clearing where brightly colored flowers adorned the grounds of a small cottage. An inviting light glowed out from the windows and smoke billowed lazily from a chimney above a thatched roof.

"Perhaps," Christopher spoke enthusiastically, "that is where I can get myself a warm meal!"

"Yes, and perhaps," the living statue added humbly, "the resident of that sanctuary will be kind enough to provide me with some advice on map reading."

In a matter of moments they were standing on the porch with Petra knocking on the door.

14
Deception at the Door

"Beware of false prophets, who come to you in sheep's clothing,
but inwardly they are ravenous wolves."
Matthew 7:15

"Hello? Is anybody home?" Petra called out hopefully.

"There is someone at the door!" a voice cawed in agitation.

"Shut up fool!" another voice scowled in a low tone. *"One more word and you will never speak again!"*

"I am coming. Give me just a minute," yet a third voice, this one much sweeter, sang out.

Christopher and Petra exchanged puzzled glances.

The door opened and before them stood an attractive woman wearing a long white dress. Dark hair crowned her head and spiraled down past sparkling blue eyes, rosy cheeks, and blossoming red lips. As her beauty captivated their eyes so, too, did her voice mesmerize their ears.

"Good afternoon," she commenced with much charm. "What a pleasant surprise it is for me, Hilda, to be paid a visit by such handsome gentlemen such as yourselves. How may I assist you?"

Succumbing to her flattery Petra bowed slightly and proceeded to his introduction.

"Good afternoon, madam," he launched politely. "I am Petra and this is my traveling companion, Christopher. Please forgive us for disturbing you but it seems we have lost our way and would be indebted to your assistance. Our map shows us…"

As Petra continued his diplomatic speech Christopher's attention was drawn to the habitation's interior that revealed a tidy and cozy room, complete with a wood table and chairs occupying its center. Nearby, a broom leaned against a hutch accommodating plates, cups, and eating utensils while the walls upheld shelves of tin canisters, glass bottles, small boxes, and many neatly arranged books, all without a hint of dust or cobwebs. In a corner, suspended from the ceiling, was an iron cage harboring a large raven whose shiny amethyst feathers testified to meticulous grooming. A stone fireplace, erupting with a kaleidoscope of flames, provoked a black cauldron to churn a medley of meat and vegetables, saturating the air with its savory bouquet. As Petra finished his discourse the tempting aroma reached the boy's nostrils, prompting his stomach to let loose one of its notorious growls.

"It appears you need more than help with directions," Hilda smiled kindly at Christopher. "Can I tempt you with some stew, young man?"

"I would give my life for a bowl," Christopher proclaimed hungrily.

"Oh, *really?*" Hilda retorted mischievously. "Please come in and have a seat."

"Well, I guess it will not do any harm to fill that cavernous belly of his," Petra smirked, wagging his head affectionately at the boy.

Closing the door behind them Petra mindfully positioned himself at a windowsill, basking his body of green stone in the sunlight. Hilda walked over to the cupboard and removed a bowl and spoon as Christopher eagerly seated himself at the table. Leaning over the scalding vat to dish up the stew, the man of stone noticed Hilda wore knee nigh ebony boots beneath her white apparel. His curiosity sparked, Petra glanced at the raven who paced along its perch in agitation, shoulders hunched, staring at him with contempt. Petra, to say the least, suddenly felt uneasy.

"Would you like some, too?" Hilda asked Petra as she sprinkled a green herb atop the steaming bowl and set it before Christopher who wasted no time in helping himself.

"No, thanks," he answered apprehensively, slapping his abdomen. "For me to eat food would be for you to eat rocks."

She nodded smugly and handed Christopher a cloth napkin.

'That green herb on Christopher's stew sure looks familiar,' Petra wondered to himself as the boy cautiously sipped another steaming spoonful.

"I have never before seen a living statue," Hilda's voice rudely interrupted his thoughts. "How did you come to have life?"

"Well, it is a bit complicated…" he stammered.

"How about just telling me why the two of you are traveling in the Lost Forest. I do not entertain many visitors you know…" Hilda trailed off suspiciously.

An enormous yawn unexpectedly broke forth from Christopher's mouth.

"I am too tired to eat another bite," he murmured, pushing the half empty bowl away from himself.

With mouth cocked open, the raven ruffled its feathers and tilted its head towards Hilda.

"Perhaps, if you could just direct us…" Petra's voice cracked.

The boy's eyes fluttered, his head wobbled, and then lacking restraint his body slumped forward onto the table.

15
Demise of the Witch

A man or a woman who is a medium, or who has familiar spirits, shall surely be put to death; they shall stone them with stones. Their blood shall be upon them.
Leviticus 20:27

For a split second no one moved and tension hung thick in the air. Petra and Hilda momentarily locked eyes, the logs in the fireplace crackled and hissed…and then the gates of Hell burst wide open! Petra watched in horror as Hilda lunged for the broom and with the touch of her hand transformed it into a sledgehammer. The raven shrieked and flapped its wings furiously as Hilda spun around to face the man of stone, her eyes flashing and throat gurgling with laughter.

The pieces of the puzzle suddenly fit into place and Petra understood the terrible truth: Hilda was a witch! Careful to remain partially bathed in the sunlight he quickly reached into the shadows and swooped up Christopher. Turning towards the door he heard an object slash through the air followed by a dull blow to his upper body,

59

knocking him off balance. Glancing back the man of stone discovered the momentum of the swing had flung Hilda to her knees but also that the sledgehammer's impact regrettably scored a crater to his left shoulder.

Without warning, the earth began to rumble, violently shaking the cottage's foundation. Fumbling for the doorknob Petra heard from behind him a thunderous crash ensued by a hideous scream. Looking back one last time he witnessed a dreadful sight: the fireplace had collapsed through the roof, crushing Hilda to death, her disheveled gray hair snaking out from beneath the rubble. The enchantment broken, books amongst the rubble now exhibited covers with devilish symbols and shattered bottles oozed vile liquids. Exiting the witch's domain Petra saw the once colorful flowers were now faded and withered, choked out by thistles and weeds.

During the next hour Petra carried Christopher through the forest and coming upon a creek followed the sparkling water upstream where he found a cave in the southern base of the Hopeful Mountains' northern range. After examining the hollow carefully Petra decided it best the boy pass the night in its seclusion and so set him gently down at the cave's entrance. The living statue then refilled the drinking flask and with his tunic blotted the Christopher's face with the cool water.

"Where are we?" Christopher mumbled drowsily.

"Thanks be to the Creator safely far from Hilda's cottage."

"I did not thank her for the delicious stew," Christopher replied, comfortably confused.

"That will not be necessary," Petra said with disgust, "for she has been smashed to smithereens."

"What happened?"

"I will tell you later but let me just say that being a master gardener I should have recognized the herb she placed on your stew as one that induces sleep. Needless to say, we escaped in the *'nick'* of time," he concluded with remorse, surveying his injury.

"Petra, you have a *'chip'* on your shoulder!" Christopher exclaimed. "Does it hurt?"

"Yes, but not physically," the man of stone answered despairingly. "It will most certainly be a reminder to me of my fallen nature. The least I could do was save your life after endangering it."

"Petra," Christopher smiled, "you are truly a gift from Heaven."

16
A Giant Discovery

But God has chosen the foolish things of the world to put to shame the wise,
and God has chosen the weak things of the world to put to shame
the things which are mighty;
1 Corinthians 1:27

The morning sun streamed throughout the wooded glen, bathing Petra's body with light and stirring him to life. Taking in the surroundings face wore on an expression of befuddlement.

"Did I not," he verbally questioned himself, "retire yesterday evening up there, at the cave's entrance?"

Boisterous inhaling and exhaling echoed out from the grotto.

"For goodness sakes," he pronounced amusingly, "that boy certainly snores loudly for being so small."

"Me? Snoring? I have been up for hours," the seed-bearer's voice pitched from behind. Petra turned to see Christopher walking through the forest, knapsack slung over his shoulder and a smile on his face.

"I awoke early," he continued, "ate breakfast and decided to wash at the river-"

"*Silence!*" Petra whispered, eyes big as saucers, pointing nervously towards the cave.

It was then a snort of irritation and movement was heard inside the hollow. The traveler's eyes bulged with fear.

"Run, Christopher, run!" Petra shouted excitedly. "I will fight it off! Just run!"

"Waaait! Do not run!" a slurred voice bellowed from the dark recess. "III will not hurt youuu!"

Christopher and Petra froze and looked anxiously up the hill. Limping slowly out from the cave was the largest man either of them had ever seen. Nearly double the height of Petra, the man was slightly hunched over, leaning heavily upon a thick oak branch of which he grasped firmly with a knotted fist. Frayed moccasins encased enormous feet while animal skins, sewn together unevenly, loosely covered his massive frame. A neck bulging with muscles erected a leathery skinned head that sprouted short black hair. Sparkling blue eyes balanced ever so carefully above a bulbous nose while below a contorted mouth part in bewilderment.

"Youuu are aliiive!" the giant marveled at seeing Petra. "When III ariiived here earlieeer this morning III thought this is aaa strange plaaace for aaa statuuue and aaa greeeeeen one at that!"

"So, you are the culprit who moved me!" Petra joked, relieved they were not only encountering a disabled giant but a friendly one as well. "For a moment I thought I had *'rocks'* in my head!"

"III did not meeean anyyy harm," the oversized man responded sheepishly. "III neeeeeeded somewhere to sleeeeeep and your bodyyy was blocking the caaave sooo III moved youuu."

At first the pilgrimaging companions found it difficult to understand the man's speech but the innocence he expressed could not be ignored. Filled with pity they offered the giant benevolence.

"Are you hungry?" Christopher asked, graciously offering the knapsack of food.

"OOOh bless youuu. That would beee niiiee," he said and taking possession of the canvas storehouse sat down upon a boulder. Scavenging through the sack he drew forth a large purple turnip and took a bite. "III have been traveling north through the Hooopeful Mountains for the past weeeeeek and have not been aaable to fiiind manyyy vegetables. III liiike vegetables."

"Where are you from?" Petra asked in curiosity.

"It is not where III am from but where III am goooing that is important," he answered with conviction. "The truth is that III am not proud of where III originaaate."

Petra gasped thinking he had perhaps offended the gentle giant. Christopher hoping to ease embarrassment vaulted into the conversation.

"You do not need to share with us-"

"It is oookaaay. III must tell myyy storyyy to all who ask sooo the Creeeaaator, His Son, and the Holyyy Breeeeeeze can beee given honor."

66

"What wonderful news!" Petra responded with joyful enthusiasm.

"III knooow it must sound odd," the giant muttered through twisted lips, "to hear of aaa giiiant who desiiires to beee maaade pure byyy the One who gives us all liiife but myyy storyyy is true and nothing short of aaa miracle."

So between bites and with complete transparency the giant shared the story of his life.

17
The Search for Truth

For since the creation of the world His invisible attributes are clearly seen, being understood by the things that are made, even His eternal power and Godhead, so that they are without excuse...professing to be wise, they became fools...and who exchanged the truth of God for the lie...
Romans 1:20, 22 & 25a

"Myyy naaame is Nathanael and III was born this waaay," he began humbly, referring to his physical handicap and speech impediment. "III am from aaa triiibe of giiiants in the South Kingdom and myyy parents diiied when III was aaa baaabyyy. Myyy aunt and uncle raaaised meee but theeey never liiiked meee much."

"I am glad not to have lived in your shoes," Petra interjected, attempting to lighten the mood, "mostly because they would not fit."

"Youuu are veryyy funnyyy!" Nathanael wheezed.

"Why did your tribe not show you any love?" Petra retorted in all seriousness. "Do they not know that someday everyone will give an account to the Creator?"

Christopher squirmed realizing he, too, needed to answer that very question.

"Well, that is the problem," Nathanael stated, this time biting into a carrot. "Youuu seeeeee, myyy triiibe worships the earth and all that has been creeeaaated rather than the Creeeaaator, Who gives us all liiife and is blessed forever. AAAmen! Anyyywaaay, as III was walking through the forest last weeeeeek feeling looonelyyy and searching for truth the Holyyy Breeeeeeze rushed through the treeeeeees and ooover myyy bodyyy giving meee understanding in that everyyyone can beee maaade new byyy the Son's blood! Scaaales were removed not onlyyy from myyy eyyyes but myyy heart also. III fell to myyy kneeeeees and praaayed,

'OOOh, Greaaat Creeeaaator, III reeepent and belieeeve! III awaaait the promise of beeeing cleansed with the blood of Your Son and empowered byyy the Holyyy Breeeeeeze tooo live riiight soooooo leeead meee this daaay in Your truth.'"

"III was instantlyyy filled with peeeace and went to share this news with the elders of myyy triiibe but theeey mocked meee for belieeeving such *faaables*. III alwaaays thought III was not welcomed but then III knew III did not beeelong sooo III left as an outcast."

Christopher's eyes glistened while Petra was unusually speechless.

"Anyyywaaay, last eeevening whiiile III was traveling through theeese woods and saw aaa small cottage in toootal disarraaay. At first III thought III would spend the niiight there but myyy spirit did not feel riiight as the plaaaace smelled of death. III turned to leeeave but heard aaa rustling noise insiiide and sooo went in to explore and found aaa raaaven, locked in aaa caaaage, its feathers in shambles and it was not in the best of moods. Out of pityyy III bent back the bars allowing the bird to escaaape."

"Although your intentions may have been good," Petra stated flatly, "I am afraid your action most likely was not."

Christopher and Nathanael winced at Petra's seemingly lack of sympathy for the ave so the man of stone proceeded to tell them what had transpired at the witch's abode.

"Thankfully neither Hilda nor the raven knew anything about the Tree of Life's seed that I carry," Christopher breathed easy, clutching the treasure inside his front jean pocket.

Before those words could dissipate into air the small party was chilled to their bones as a shrieking caw sounded in the branches overhead. Wings flapping wildly the raven rose into the sky, brazenly mocking the travelers below.

18
Campfire Companions

Though one may be overpowered by another, two can withstand him.
And a threefold cord is not quickly broken.
Ecclesiastes 4:12

"I had a feeling that bird was a dirty one!" Petra uttered in disgust.

"We had best be on the move," Christopher stated with concern. "Let us not forget that our mission is of utmost urgency."

"Could yooou pleeease tell meee where yoooou are goooing and what it has to do with aaa seeeeeed?" Nathanael asked in frustration.

"Please forgive us!" Petra begged the giant. "You have been ever so kind to share with us your story and yet we have not shown you the common courtesy. I am Petra and this is my traveling companion, Christopher. We will be happy to answer all your questions but must do so while journeying on the road for I fear our undertaking has now been jeopardized."

The small party set off in a southeasterly direction but due to Nathanael's physical impairment traveling was slow and at times challenging. Christopher and Petra were considerate in assisting the giant along the way and while doing so relayed to him their individual stories and the reason for their plight.

"I can assure you," Petra concluded his narrative, "we can never be at peace with the Creator unless we accept the gift of forgiveness which comes only through the blood of His Son."

"Myyy desiiire is to ooobeeey the Holyyy Breeeeeeze too!" the giant exclaimed. "Byyy the waaay, when do weee plant the seeeeeed and eeeat the fruit to reeeeeeeive everlasting liiife?"

"I am not sure," the man of stone answered honestly, "but you can be certain the Creator will make that known to us when it is time."

"Are youuu not excited about beeeing cleansed and given new liiife?" Nathanael queried Christopher, eyes full of compassion.

"Well," the boy paused, slightly irritated, "all I care about is completing this good deed so I can be reunited with my friends."

"It must beee niiice to have friends," the giant responded gingerly, realizing he had touched Christopher's soft spot.

"You no longer need to worry about having people who care for and love you," Petra chimed in, patting the giant's back and bringing a smile to his ginormous face.

Hours later all three arrived at a thick grove of trees atop a ridge. Open land stretched out below them to the east, giving affirmation they had finally conquered the Lost Forest. It was in the solitude and protection of the trees they decided to camp for the night.

"This will be a good place to stop," Petra said with satisfaction. "We can relax here tonight and navigate across the fields to the East Kingdom tomorrow. With the smell of rain in the air I believe the both of you might be interested in building a campfire."

As the sun prepared to set the sky became crowded with dark clouds. Christopher and Nathanael collected branches and twigs while Petra fenced off a broad clearing with rocks and commenced rubbing two sticks together under some kindling. The fire was soon blazing and the boy and giant basked in the warmth, partaking of delectable provisions from Samuel's garden. Petra then prepared for his nightly hibernation by posturing himself in a standing position.

"I have been meaning to ask you," Christopher began with hesitancy, "why do you stand rather than sit at night?"

"I am made of stone, correct?" Petra commented with pride.

The boy nodded in confusion.

"Well, only a statue sculpt from rotting pumpkins would ever sit or lay down!"

"Heee is hilariiious!" Nathanael roared.

At those jesting words the sun leapt over the world's end, leaving the man of stone lifeless and smiling from ear to ear. With stomachs filled and bodies resting comfortably, the remaining two reclined to the sound of rain falling softly upon the canopy of branches above. Just prior to drifting off into a peaceful slumber Christopher anticipated soon being reunited with the twelve he cherished most.

19
Beneath the Earth

"Again I say to you that if two of you agree on earth concerning anything that they ask, it will be done for them by My Father in Heaven."
Matthew 18:19

The ringing in Nathanael's ears was like the irritating hum of a mosquito. He swatted the air clumsily, grunted in frustration, and rolled over in search of his quickly fading dream of vegetables. His blue eyes then shot wide open and his immense body sat up. The disturbance was much worse than the nuisance of an insect buzzing for it was Petra's voice yelling throughout the forest.

"Christopher! Christopher!" the living statue hollered frantically.

"Whyyy all the noise?" the giant asked in distress.

"Christopher has been kidnapped and the seed stolen!"

"III am to blaaame!" Nathanael scolded himself. "III was sooo tiiired last niiight III would have slept through the end of the world!"

"No one is more at fault than I," Petra whined in desperation, glancing shamefully at his shoulder. "All I know is that if we had any more *'pities'* we could throw a party. It seems beasts smelling of spoiled eggs have taken our friend to what hideous place I cannot imagine."

Cloven prints littered the dampened ground and a putrid odor lingered in the air. He wrinkled up his enormous nose and grimaced in disgust.

"All the clues lead northwest, back toward the Hopeful Mountains," Petra affirmed.

The searchers quickly gathered their belongings and trekked until coming to a narrow passage that lead into a short and desolate dead-end canyon.

"I believe we are about to enter the valley of the shadow of death," Petra declared sullenly.

"Well, III am readyyy," Nathanael spoke bravely, tightening his grip on the makeshift cane, "III have myyy staff and it will not bece aaa comfort to the beeeasts who took Christooopher."

Nearing the channel's far boundary they discovered overgrown grass recently trampled by cloven hooves and a great cavity in the ground with a sign next to it that read:

THE STAIRWELL

Enter the Emperor's domain at your own risk...

for you may not have the option to leave!

Looking down they were startled to find that a circular staircase, hewn out from the earth, spiraled downward into the gloom while rising unmercifully upward was the offensive stench of sulfur.

"There is only one thing to do so I ask you please, do not drop me," Petra pleaded, squeezing the giant's muscular arm.

"Do youuu want meee to carryyy youuu down there?"

"Well, I will not be able to walk myself," the man of stone spoke matter-of-factly, "for I can assure you the sun will not be shining in that pit."

Petra walked over to a nearby tree and pruned a branch from its trunk, stripping it of twigs and leaves began rummaging through his knapsack.

"Do me a favor, Nathanael," his muffled voice could be heard from inside the canvas bag, "tear off the sleeves from your shirt."

Perplexity anointed the giant's face.

"Here it is!" Petra exclaimed, holding up a glass vial. "This oil is just what we need."

Nathanael's body slouched over more than usual, mouth gaping wide with misunderstanding.

"What are you waiting for?" Petra inquired impatiently. "If we are to find Christopher we must launch our descent right away."

With blind obedience Nathanael tugged half-heartedly at his shirt sleeves.

"Can you see in the dark?" the man of stone asked in playful irritation.

Nathanael shook his head.

"I did not think so," the man of stone laughed at the colossal man's confusion. "The torch I am making will provide you light where there is none."

Finally comprehending Nathanael promptly tore at his furry raiment and handed it to the living statue. Wrapping the animal skins tightly around the branch's end Petra proceeded by soaking it with oil. Nathanael then struck two stones together close to the assemblage, sparking the portable beacon to life.

"Here's the plan," Petra said while reaching for the giant's cane with one hand and securing the torch in his other, "you will carry me beneath the earth, rescue Christopher, and deliver us all back here to the land of light and the living."

Nathanael nodded though the task weighed heavily upon him in more ways than one.

"May the Creator safely guide your every step," Petra added with grace, "and may our little friend's heart be softened for repentance."

The giant hoisted Petra over his broad shoulder and responded, "Indeeeeeed, and maaay His Son and the Holyyy Breeeeeze proootect us until weee can fellooowship again."

The smile on Petra's face froze as Nathanael stepped down around the first curve of stairs and out of the sunshine. After numerous rotations he began to suffer due to the statue's weight as well as the Stairwell's environmental conditions: the repulsive fetor was nauseating but the humidity, quite frankly, was unbearable and it wasn't long until the giant was drenched in sweat. Resting occasionally he adjusted his grip on the statue and steadfastly continued the descent, eventually reaching bedrock.

Shuffling along a muggy corridor Nathanael soon progressed through an arched portal where a narrow walkway spanned a great cavern, walls and ceiling glowing red. Inching across the bridge he timidly peeked down into the abyss to see a lake of fire, hissing and bubbling, the haze stinging his blue eyes and charring his face with ash. Reaching the far side a prayer of gratitude poured from his lips.

Despite his strength Nathanael's muscles eventually cramped from and so standing Petra up proceeded to drink long and thirstily from the water flask. Wiping perspiration from his brow the giant groaned with exhaustion.

"Maaay the Creeeaaator have mercyyy on meee and give meee His strength-"

'WHOOOOOOOSSSSSHHHH!' came the sound of an object swinging through the air.

Petra's torch flickered and an excruciating pain riveted through Nathanael's head...and then he knew no more!

20
Prisoners of the Dark Emperor

I cried out to the LORD because of my affliction, and He answered me.
Out of the belly of Sheol I cried, and You heard my voice.
Jonah 2:2-3a

Christopher sat on a hard dirt floor, crying in the dark. His tears, however, had nothing to do with being awakened in the dead of night, blindfolded, gagged, and shackled by two obnoxious characters who not only smelled like rotten eggs but who had continuously made coarse jokes about the disabled giant and man of stone. They were not associated with the sensation of falling backwards in slow motion down an endless hole, the sweltering heat, nor from being held hostage in a vault whose iron door after being slammed shut had continued pealing in his ears. His tears did not even have to do with the monotony of what seemed like days in this pit nor the countless hours of restless sleep. Rather, the sorrow which had arisen in the attic came haunting again, unbeknownst to him in the earth's belly.

"Now I will never again see my friends," he sobbed aloud.

"If you need a friend, I am here," a tender voice spoke from out of the darkness.

Struggling, Christopher managed to tug the blindfold down below his eyes in hopes of identifying the propagator of kindness but only discovered blackness abounded all the more.

"It will take some time but your sight will acclimate to the gloom," it reassured cheerfully.

"How can you be happy as a prisoner in this dungeon?" Christopher asked spitefully.

"On the contrary, never have I been so free," was the truthful response. "I am content knowing the Creator, His Son, and the Holy Breeze will, at the appointed time, deliver me. May I ask, why are you not satisfied with the trial given you?"

Living in denial, Christopher blamed the Creator for separating him from his friends. Rather than repenting of selfishness he instead continued to believe that the *good work* of delivering the

84

seed would be the reward by which he enjoyed a reunion with his twelve friends.

Like Petra and Nathanael, this unseen individual sought to please the Creator and this pricked the boy's heart. Although Monday cautioned prudence in sharing about the seed here was an opportunity for Christopher to vent his frustration. Besides, he most likely would be spending his remaining days of life in this dreadful pit.

"Well," Christopher grunted, slightly abashed, "it is rather a very long story-"

"Although time is a finite amenity," the voice smiled audibly, "I do not believe we need to be worried about running out of it just yet."

With that last statement Christopher disclosed all the events of the past few days and when mentioning the witch's cottage a sigh of remorse broke through the darkness.

"Did she mention her name as being *'Hilda'*?" it asked gravely.

"Why, yes," Christopher answered in amazement. "How did you know?"

"I will tell you," came the regretful reply, "but please, first continue with your story."

Throughout Christopher's narrative the voice gestured verbal encouragement and when his story concluded the boy felt as if a great burden had been lifted from his spirit.

"Just as you have been kind to share with me," the voice commented gracefully, "so, too, will I tell you about myself."

Keeping its promise, the voice ministered to Christopher in love.

21
A Humble Confession

Therefore humble yourselves under the mighty hand of God,
that He may exalt you in due time, casting all your care upon Him,
for He cares for you.
1 Peter 5:6-7

"A long time ago I lived in a beautiful village in the North Kingdom where the people feared the Creator and expectantly awaited the promise of everlasting life through His Son. I, however, was rebellious to those notions and so lived narcissistic and carefree along with twin sisters whom I considered friends. I am deeply saddened to hear you recently met one of them. Their names were Hazel and Hilda," the voice paused as Christopher gasped with astonishment.

"Both sisters were receiving instruction in the art of witchcraft from Nimrod, the chief servant of the Dark Emperor, of whose dungeon we are both now imprisoned."

A cold chill raced up the boy's spine.

"Hazel and Hilda practiced magic to impress me and I was flattered by their romantic endeavors. The alchemy they first exercised was simple and seemingly harmless: Hazel would change stones to bread for me and Hilda would mend my torn garments with the touch of her hand. However, with all undertakings that do not bring honor to the Creator their knowledge of devilry increased and their thirst for evil was aroused. As their training in magic reached darker levels I realized any affections they may have once entertained for me had instead become a bitter rivalry between themselves and so when malice towards one another grew I fled southwest, humiliated and dejected."

"Many years passed but the Creator began softening my heart, provoking within me a desire to pursue righteousness. If I was to be shown mercy and obtain grace I must first abandon my pride and ask forgiveness from Hazel and Hilda for the resentment I harbored towards them. They, too, needed the Creator's love and so with a penitent heart I resolved to speak with them, regardless the cost," the voice confessed, evoking guilt in Christopher's heart.

"After some days of traveling I arrived in my hometown and lodged with an old acquaintance. During supper that evening I learned that months earlier the town's crops had withered and died. Rather than praying to the Creator for help the people had sought *'good'* witch Hilda's aid who then sprinkled magic powder on their fields and gardens, restoring new life to their fruits and vegetables!"

"Unbeknownst to me, during that very meal I was eating the magically tampered fruit and vegetables, leading my heart to once again pursue my fallen nature: denying the Creator as my source of life, arrogantly believing I had no need of cleansing by His Son's blood, and feeling apathetic towards the Holy Breeze in sanctifying me...all common traits of those enslaved by the Dark Emperor!"

Christopher gasped realizing those attributes embodied his life.

"Kneeling at my bed that night I cried out to the Creator for help and waking the next morning discovered the Holy Breeze sweeping throughout the village, purifying everyone's heart from the poison and renewing them to again serve the Creator! We all then witnessed another miracle ensue: rising up out of the ground in the fields and gardens was a new harvest of larger, brighter in color, and better tasting fruits and vegetables...swallowing Hilda's crops whole!"

"You are to blame for this!"

"The angry voice ravishing the air belonged to Hilda. She scurried towards me, her body draped in a black robe and crippled due to the effects of practicing magic. Her skin, a dull gray, the color of death, was covered with warts while knotted hair, hanging limply about a wrinkled face, framed a gnarled mouth of chipped teeth. Eyes yellow with disease she glared hatefully at me."

"I am to blame? It is the evil in your heart that gives birth to your wicked deeds! Repent and trust in the Creator before it is too late!"

"Nonsense! You and these people will suffer the consequences for resisting the Dark Emperor!" Come with me now!"

"Clenching my wrist with her icy fingers I willingly accompanied her hoping she would not harm the village residents. For the remainder of the day she jostled me through the woods, cursing and grumbling, vowing I would give an account of my foolishness to Nimrod. I, on the other hand, repeatedly urged her to repent and choose life but she refused to listen. At sunset we reached a short valley whereby two hideous goat-men reeking of sulfur shackled and chained me, pulling my body down a staircase into the earth."

"Hilda, I forgive you!"

"I do not need to be forgiven!"

Hearing how the witch had scoffed Samuel the seed-bearer lowered his head and remained silent.

"I never saw her again but now I know that she, being one of the Exiles, will forever suffer miserably for rejecting truth." The voice added somberly, "I wasted much of my life spurning the Creator's love. Please, I beg you, do not make the same mistake."

Taking a deep breath the youth raised his head and with conviction responded with honesty.

"Your words have been a balm to my troubled heart, urging me to consider what is important in light of eternity."

Outside the dungeon voices were now heard howling wickedly as keys jingled at the iron lock.

"Before we are led off to face what horrors I cannot imagine, may I ask," Christopher begged with anticipation, "who are you?"

The prison door was violently thrust open and two goat-men staggered in, bringing with them a fresh wave of foulness. Light from their torches bathed the cell's walls, revealing the person behind the voice: a dark blue robe swaddled an elderly man, head bald though a long white beard hung patiently down upon his chest. Despite hands and feet being shackled he was indeed free and that was evident in his eyes that twinkled with the hope of everlasting life.

"My name is Samuel."

22
Trials and Temptations

Trust in the LORD with all your heart, and lean not on your own understanding;
in all your ways acknowledge Him, and He shall direct your paths.
Proverbs 3:5-6

"On your feet!" a goat-man shouted gruffly. "It is time for you to pay respect to Nimrod!"

Christopher and Samuel were pulled to their feet and led out of the dungeon and down a tunnel that sloped further into the earth.

"Why did you not tell Petra where you were going?" he questioned the elderly man, stunned by his identity.

"Out of shame," Samuel confessed. "Besides, I thought my absence from home would be brief. How glad I am to know my friend of stone has accompanied you along the way. My prayers are that he is now safe for I long to see him again."

"Save your breath for the one who is worthy of it," the second monster growled menacingly.

"Only the Creator-" Samuel began unashamedly.

"*Silence!*" the beast shouted, waving its torch dangerously near the old man's beard.

Traversing throughout numerous sultry passageways Christopher and Samuel were finally ushered into a large vaulted chamber where their hearts were filled with both joy and sorrow. Between two goat-men and bound in chains was Nathanael, his enormous frame soaked with perspiration and kneeling submissively upon the hard soil in a state of exhaustion. Blood from a gash on the crown of his head trickled between his eyes of which were just now coming to focus on the boy.

"Christooopher! Youuu are oookaaay!" he barked with joy from the side of his twisted mouth. One of the beasts savagely jabbed the gentle giant in the ribs causing him to groan in pain and gasp for air.

A short distance from Nathanael stood Petra, motionless and naive to his surroundings. The man of stone continued to faithfully

94

uphold Nathanael's cane and the torch he himself had made, selflessly sharing its light with all. Upon seeing his beloved statue Samuel's eyes overflowed with tears of thanksgiving to the Creator.

The blissful reunion, however, was short-lived for off to Petra's left was an iron throne on which sat the most wretched creature imaginable. A body of brown decaying flesh clung to protruding bones, eagerly seeking to penetrate the rancid skin. Hanging limply from either side of its spine were a pair of tattered wings. Gold bracelets set with colorful jewels dangled loosely from emaciated wrists while yellow claws, splintered from negligence, curled upon themselves. An oblong head void of hair featured pointed ears, a repulsive pug nose, ashen eyes, and a black slit for a mouth.

"Welcome to the Underworld," it shrieked. "I am Nimrod and this is the domain of my master, the Dark Emperor, of whom will conquer the Creator, His Son, and the Holy Breeze," and it was at these words he cringed in disgust with the mention of those blessed names. "Not far below us the Exiles await the Day of Judgment," he sneered with satisfaction. "Prior to your sentencing let me make one thing clear: I know who you are and what you possess, you might say a *'little bird'* told me," he snarled, flapping his wings feebly. "By the way, do you like my new *'lamp stand'* ?" he snickered, pointing a disjointed finger at Petra.

"What are *you*?" Christopher spoke up bravely, abhorred by the vile creature.

"Aaaah, seed-bearer, I am a fallen angel of course!" he belched arrogantly. "I take great delight knowing my decision to rebel against the Creator has given Him sorrow!"

Although Christopher could not fathom the hostility of that remark it grieved both Nathanael and Samuel.

"You first, old man," the fallen angel addressed Samuel disrespectfully. "It is you who unraveled Hilda's magic, restored the crops and by doing so uprooted the ignorance, arrogance, and apathy she planted in the people's hearts of the North Kingdom. Due to this injustice perpetrated against my master and taking into consideration

96

your age," he belittled him, "you will be locked away as my permanent guest here in the bowels of the earth."

"I accept your decree," Samuel responded, joy radiating from his face. "If it is here in the world of the dead that I am to await the promise of life everlasting then so be it."

"As for you, retarded fool," Nimrod jeered at Nathanael while ignoring Samuel's comment, "since you assisted both the man of stone and boy in their endeavors your punishment will be to dig a thousand more tunnels here in the Underworld."

Eyes downcast, the sleeveless giant remained silent in the seat of unjust condemnation. Licking his cracked lips with satisfaction Nimrod directed his attention fully upon Christopher.

"Young man," he began in flattery but quickly progressed to sarcasm, "I know which world you call home. My master has other servants there who are now busily misleading many to pursue selfish ambitions, distracting them during their brief and pitiful lives." Nimrod leaned forward and lowered his voice, breath molesting the air,

"Little boy, my master has been seeking to obtain fruit from the Tree of Life since the Fall. Where are you taking the seed?"

"To the king and queen in the East kingdom-"

"I despise that stubborn couple of royalty!" Nimrod whined. "They and their people have continuously refused to heed my authority and have instead remained steadfast, hoping in the Creator's false promises. I take great pleasure," he squealed in ecstasy, "knowing at this very moment the people of that kingdom are being pierced with a terrible pang!"

Regaining his composure he sat back and snarled, "What will be your reward for completing this *good deed* of delivering the seed?"

"I was hoping to see my friends," the boy responded sheepishly.

"Were you promised by the Creator a reunion with those you cherish?"

"Well, not exactly..."

"You have hoped in vain!" the demon threw back his grotesque head and snorted. Amusing himself with the jeweled bracelets the

98

Dark Emperor's servant cocked his head and spoke in a sweet sticky voice, "Give me the seed and I will take you to your twelve friends now, to be with forever."

"Forever?" Christopher echoed dreamily.

"Forever," the fallen angel moaned hungrily, believing the Creator's plans would soon be thwarted.

Pulling the wood box from his pocket Christopher unlatched the lid and opened it, revealing prickly thorns covered with crimson love. Emanating from the seed was a wholesome and invigorating fragrance, instantly purifying the stale air.

As Christopher reached out to offer the precious treasure the Holy Breeze suddenly and swiftly entered the chamber, breathing courage into the boy's heart, empowering him to renounce his selfish rebellion.

Christopher looked straight into Nimrod's pallid eyes and boldly proclaimed,

"I choose to keep the seed!"

23
The Children of Light

Nimrod's pleasant demeanor immediately turned sour. Ever since Samuel and Nathanael had shown contentment by accepting without dispute the future he determined for them, a fiery rage had been kindling within his forsaken soul. Now that a boy had the nerve to refuse his rare offer of generosity the boiling volcano of anger was about to erupt. Furious, Nimrod stood up and shouted.

"Unless you give me the seed you will rot in my dungeons!"

"That is not fair!" Christopher responded in a fluster.

"I do not play fair!" the fallen angel snapped.

Shutting the lid and latching it with emphasis Christopher tucked the vessel safely back into his pocket.

"I *still* choose to keep the seed!"

"Back to the dungeons!" Nimrod screamed.

As the goat-men roughed Nathanael to his feet and jerked Samuel and Christopher towards the arched portal an unforeseen event occurred: the sweet sound of a cappella singing could be faintly heard throughout the Underworld. Intensifying by the moment, a bright and cheerful melody of beautiful harmonization, void of words, undeniably conveyed a message of victorious love.

"Oh, no!" Nimrod cried. "The Children of Light!"

The hoofed servants of the Dark Emperor fell to their knees cowering, hands over their eyes and bodies trembling.

Materializing through the walls were eight children, four boys paired to four girls, all dressed in robes of translucent white, bodies illuminating the chamber with radiant light. Not missing a single note the first boy and girl couple touched the seed-bearer's shackles and the iron restraints promptly fell to the ground. Other pairs released Samuel and Nathanael from their fetters in like manner while the last boy and girl tenderly clutched Petra's wrists and without exertion ascended with the man of stone passing uninhibited through the ceiling above! The remaining six children similarly paired, grasped Christopher, Samuel, and Nathanael then subsequently arose, penetrating the earth's crust, leaving behind the dimension of substance. Everything now transparent including their own bodies, the four former prisoners looked down through the soil to see Nimrod having a temper tantrum with the goat-men fleeing him in fear.

Looking to his left and right Christopher exchanged smiles of astonishment and relief with Samuel and Nathanael. In the twinkling of an eye, a foretaste of the Resurrection, the party broke through the rich topsoil and found themselves standing beneath mammoth green stems and a canopy of humongous flowers. It was late afternoon and as the Children of Light released their hands and submerged back into the earth, their song of deliverance fading softly away.

"Thanks to the Creator," the man of stone sighed appreciatively, "I am no longer 'petra-fied' and have been graciously set amongst enormous scented hyacinths, lavender, honeysuckle-"

"Is that how you greet an *old* friend?" Samuel interrupted Petra playfully.

The statue turned to see his earthly master standing with arms open wide, face beaming with joy.

"Samuel!"

Casting down the torch and Nathanael's walking stick Petra embraced his beloved and loyal friend with a rock hug.

"I had cursed the Creator," Samuel stated with regret, "but out of grace He blessed me with you."

"We have been rescued after being three days in the depths of Sheol," Christopher expressed gratefully.

"Indeed, and He has heard my prayers concerning you," the man of stone responded with affection, "for you were *heavy* on my heart."

"Speeeaking of *heavyyy*," the giant smirked, stooping down to retrieve his walking stick, "the next tiiime III have to carryyy youuu could youuu pleeease first gooo on aaa diiiet?"

"Are you alright?!" Petra asked Nathanael, concerned at seeing the giant's face covered with dried blood.

"OOOh, yes, III am. Myyy onlyyy reeegret," he answered, patting his scalp gingerly, "is that III was not born with aaa hard head liiike youuu!"

With that comment everyone laughed until bellies ached.

24
Revenge of the Raven

Beloved, do not avenge yourselves, but rather give place to wrath;
for it is written, "Vengeance is Mine, I will repay," says the Lord.
Romans 12:19

Once Samuel and Nathanael were properly introduced each person relayed his story to the others regarding what had transpired while apart during the last few days and in Samuel's case weeks. It was not long until Christopher's stomach once again growled.

"Where is the knapsack?" he asked inquisitively. "I am famished."

"The deeemons stole it after theeey knocked meee on the 'noggin," Nathanael responded in dismay.

"Unfortunately, the map is missing too," Petra voiced sullenly.

"Perhaps that is a good thing," Samuel teased his friend of stone. "Maneuvering east through this enlarged vegetation, however, should take us to the palace in the East Kingdom."

"He is right," Christopher chimed with enthusiasm. "Besides, what truly matters is that we still have the seed," he said and withdrew the coffer from his pocket. Handling it clumsily, the seed-bearer lost hold on the Creator's gift of life and it slipped between his fingers, tumbling to the ground.

That split second blunder was just enough time for the group's worst nightmare to occur: an amethyst winged form stormed from the sky, swooped up the box with razor-sharp claws and alighted upon the frond of a monstrous flower, disheveled feathers and all.

"You fools! Did you really think you could escape from Nimrod with the seed to the Tree of Life?" the raven taunted them from above.

"Hilda's fowl!" Petra cried aloud.

"Oh, no, I am much worse than that!" the bird screeched with disdain. "Do you not know who I am, 'rock-head'?" it sassily mocked the man of stone.

"Shame on you," Samuel answered, shaking his head in disgust. "Only I would know who you are, Hazel."

"How did you figure me out?   It must be my delightful personality!" her shiny black beak snapped sarcastically.

"Hazel? Hilda's twin sister?" Christopher asked in shock.

"So young and yet so smart," she sneeringly cocked her head.

"How did youuu beeecome aaa bird?" Nathanael asked innocently.

"Well, since I now have all the time in the world," Hazel scoffed, referring to the prize she clung to, "I will tell you. Once upon a time my hag of a sister and I were friends with a *'youthful'* man," her beady eyes glared at Samuel, "but our game of impressing him turned to defeating one another with magic."

"I have since forgiven-" Samuel began tenderly.

"Quiet!   I am telling a story!" Hazel retorted angrily.   "After consulting Nimrod for mystical powers, each new trick we learned festered our hatred for one another. Days after *'old white beard'* skipped town Hilda reached a deeper level of witchcraft than I and changed me into this despicable bird," she crowed with scorn.   "We then

107

migrated to the Lost Forest where she conjured up a shanty, locked me in an iron cage, and until her demise served the Dark Emperor."

The party of four exchanged disheartened glances.

"Months ago and upon Nimrod's request Hilda returned to our hometown and corrupted the people's crops," Hazel continued. "Anyway, about a week ago the *old man* ruined everything by exposing the Dark Emperor's plan and upon hearing the news, my sister traveled to the North Kingdom and seized the perpetrator, delivering him to Nimrod. Upon returning to our shack she cursed,

'I will destroy the people of the North Kingdom once and for all!'"

She proceeded by altering our dwelling into a cottage in the event the townsfolk had followed her home. She then deceitfully transformed herself from a hag into a beautiful woman and began preparing a poisonous stew to offer as a gift to the people of our village in the North Kingdom."

"The stew was poisonous?" Petra asked in alarm, looking apprehensively at Christopher.

"Your arrival," Hazel scolded Petra, "interrupted her before she could finish adding all the deadly ingredients."

"What was she going to do with us?" Christopher inquired nervously.

"You were to be cast into the stew making it more flavorful but the man of stone was to be pulverized into dust and spread to the wind!"

"What about the seeeeeed?" Nathanael slurred.

"Although she knew nothing of that when the boy and statue visited the cottage, upon finding it in their possession Hilda would have sowed it in the richest soil and once grown to maturity, eaten its fruit and lived forever...with me as her everlasting slave!" Hazel's feathers shuddered. "Thanks to you, oversized oaf, I have escaped with my life!"

"Why did you not revert back to human form after Hilda's death?" Petra wondered audibly. "Like the cottage's decay, should not the spell on you have been cancelled with her downfall?"

"I thank my lucky stars that did not happen for if it had I would have been cramped to death in that miserable cage," the raven expressed a rare act of appreciation. "During those long years of captivity I made every attempt to reverse the spell and restore myself to human form but to no avail. The particular spell she cast was one by which can only be altered by another living individual."

"I am guessing you still serve the Dark Emperor?" Samuel presumed with remorse.

"My *friend* how wise you are! Once freed from my iron prison I flew straight to Nimrod and relayed everything to him including my eavesdropping on you three buffoons. I begged for restoration but being more useful to him as a bird, Nimrod vowed to change me if I obtained for him the coveted seed. Now that I have accomplished that task," Hazel cackled wickedly, "I will now return to the Underworld and receive what is due to me: restoration and life everlasting!"

"Confess all your rebellious pride and seek forgiveness from the Creator before it is too late!" Samuel pleaded.

"Heavens, no! I am in control of my own destiny!" she boasted arrogantly.

"What about-" Petra began.

"Enough of these questions!" Hazel rudely scolded him. "It is time for me to go!"

At that last impatient remark the raven flapped her wings wildly and rose high into the air, cawing with mockery, claws clutching tightly the Creator's gift of love.

25
Honeycomb Haven

My Son, eat honey because it is good,
and the honeycomb which is sweet to your taste;
Proverbs 24:13

With an expression of despair Samuel cried out, "Only the Creator can help us now!"

No a single one of them doubted that unquestionable truth but all were surprised when it occurred!

Cresting the petals of a nearby orange poppy was the largest honeybee any one of them could ever imagine existing. Crystalline wings beat at a dizzying pace, generating a perpetual roar and lifting the insect's three black and yellow body sections into the early evening sky. A robust abdomen, furry and filled with nectar, flaunted a deadly stinger as jointed legs, covered in pollen, protruded from a sturdy midsection. Its head, featuring a set of razor-sharp mandibles and pair of ebony antennae, explored the environs with two multifaceted orbs.

Without question, the honeybee's unexpected appearance terrified the raven. Fearing for her life, Hazel abruptly changed directions mid-flight and consequently lost her grip on the precious vessel, causing it to somersault through the air and land intact at Christopher's feet. As he quickly picked up the priceless treasure and tucked it into his front pocket, Hazel's raspy caw could be faintly heard cursing as she sped angrily towards Nimrod's realm. The travelers though grateful to have the seed again were not similarly blessed with a way of escape.

"It looks as if we have jumped out of the frying pan and into the fire," Petra yelled over the whirring noise.

Bracing for what was sure to be their doom everyone bowed their heads in prayer. As the droning peaked and the gust from vibrating wings reached hurricane proportions the clamor unexpectedly ceased. One by one the companions opened their eyes and looked up to behold an amazing sight: the gargantuan insect knelt before them...head likewise bowed in prayer!

"Juzzzt like me I hope your prayerzzz have been anzzzwered," the honeybee buzzed in a friendly tone, peering at the party through its myriad of eyes.

"Nooo doubt theeey have been," Nathanael sighed in relief. "It seeeeeems that youuu and III share the saaame struggle," the giant added referring to their speech.

"Yezzz, yezzz, we mozzzt zzzertainly do!" the honeybee exclaimed happily.

"What was it that you 'bee-seeched' the Creator for in prayer?" Petra quipped.

"The Creator'zzz ZZZon told Queen Bernizzze and her honeybeezzz including myzzzelf, Blozzzzzzzom, to be on the lookout for Hizz zzzervantzzz who are traveling with the gloriouzzz zzzeed from the Tree of Life. If found, we are to fly them to our colony where they can be refrezzzhed. My prayer wazzz that you are the onezzz."

"We are!" Christopher smiled. "When can we leave? I am ready for some refreshment!"

With the exception of Petra they were utterly exhausted, drenched in sweat, reeking of sulfur, and smeared with dirt.

"I will zzzignal for zzzome of my fellow workerzzz to come and azzzzzzzizzzt me in tranzzzporting you to the honeycomb."

Blossom began humming a delightful tune when there came soaring over the horizon three mammoth-sized bees, legs laden with pollen, bellies full of nectar. Moments later all four arthropods stood at attention waiting to carry the party of four to the honeycomb haven.

"Do not be bazzzhful! Pleazzze, climb aboard!" Blossom buzzed gracefully.

Having experienced air flight Christopher led the way by stepping upon one of Blossom's limbs, hoisting himself up by her woolly cloak, and straddling her about the neck. The remaining three followed suit, conquering their own flying steeds.

"Grazzzp onto uzzz tightly!" Blossom gave the command and with the smoothest of launches Christopher and company ascended into the fragrant drenched sky. The view from their heightened elevation revealed expansive fields blooming with dazzling colored flowers.

It was not long until the entourage approached a dense cluster of dark green vines, coiling about in every direction and bearing an abundance of ripe blackberries. As the four honeybees plunged amongst the vegetation, weaving their way between leaves and thistles, their passengers found themselves inside a vast hollowed bramble visible by the golden hour's light. Suspended from the living canopy was a colossal beehive whereby hundreds of honeybees darted in and out of the clay edifice's underside, buzzing happily and depositing their precious liquid of gold into vaults of wax. Beneath it all a stream flowed and it was there the travelers were first taken.

"Onzzze you have wazzzhed up," Blossom began cheerfully, "we will enter the beehive where you may eat your fill of honey and zzzleep the night in the comfort of a honeycomb. Early tomorrow morning we will tranzzzport you to the palazzze of the king and queen in the Eazzzt Kingdom."

The water was invigorating and everyone rejoiced as the grime and sweat were scrubbed away. His heart overflowing with joy Nathanael hummed along with the honeybees.

"Oh, Nathanael," Petra called anticipatory, washing dust out from the crater on his shoulder.

"That is meee," the large man responded melodically.

"You could not carry a tune if you held it with both hands!"

Before the man of stone could dodge out of the way he was dripping wet, compliments of a splash from his oversized friend that provoked all to laugh at their banter.

Clean and rejuvenated the pilgrims mounted their behemoth rides and were escorted upwards through the commune's oval entrance. Crystals embedded within terra cotta walls illuminated the interior, revealing tiered ledges. The insects danced their guests down a corridor comprised of hexagon chambers, sealed with delicious elixir.

"Conzzzume azzz much honey azzz you like and zzzleep in thozzze empty vaultzzz over there," she pointed with her antennae.

117

Once the three had disembarked Petra's honeybee questioned why the man of stone did not. Realizing his stalwart grip was all that had prevented the lifeless man of green from falling off his ride, Samuel provided an explanation to the bees.

"Bezzzzzz will stay with you tonight zzzo the zzztatue can rezzzt," Blossom replied. "May you all zzzleep well with the blezzzzzzzingzzz of the Creator, Hizzz ZZZon, and the Holy Breezzze."

Blossom and the two other bees shuffled down the hallway as Bess commenced the vigil, easing her large frame into a kneeling position upon the clay floor. With his walking stick Nathanael punctured a small hole in the top of a nearby cell enabling himself, Christopher, and Samuel to partake of the wholesome treat. Eating to their heart's content the three then climbed into chambers of soft warm wax and without a care in the world slept the night away in serenity.

26
A Royal Surprise

Beloved, let us love one another, for love is of God;
and everyone who loves is born of God and knows God.
He who does not love does not know God, for God is love.
1 John 4:7-8

Christopher looked groggily out from his vault to find Samuel kneeling in prayer and Nathanael occupying himself with licking a remnant of honey from his fingertips. Bess balanced the rigid form of Petra upon her back while grooming her antennae with great attentiveness. The seed-bearer squirmed out of his cell and obliged himself to the endless supply of liquid gold.

"Good morning, travelerzzz," Blossom greeted them cheerfully, accompanied by two other bees. "Although time rezzztrainzzz uzzz for a vizzzit with her majezzzty, Queen Bernizzze zzzendzzz her blezzzzzzingzzz azzz you embark in zzzervice for the Creator."

"Please thank her for the generous hospitality," spoke Samuel, rising to his feet. "We hope to someday make her acquaintance."

119

Once again sitting atop their steeds the four were escorted down a corridor of clay and descended in flight through the hive's lower aperture, abruptly embraced by the dawn's light.

"What a glorious morning!" Petra proclaimed, awaking to life.

"Good morning to youuu, Mr. Rotting Pumpkin!" Nathanael hollered, jesting his friend of stone.

"Why do you call me 'Mr. Rotting Pumpkin'?" the living statue asked in puzzlement.

"Youuu once told meee that aaa statuuue who sits or laaays down must beee maaade of rotting pumpkins sooo III am onlyyy taaaking youuu at your word!"

Buzzing with laughter the honeybees swiftly maneuvered their riders above a patchwork quilt landscape of houses, barns, and grain fields. Ahead, a white castle sat upon a hill, full of splendor with flags of blue and green unfurled, casting long shadows upon towers and parapets in the early morning light. At the stronghold's center was a broad courtyard and at its center a fountain of which cascaded into a large pool. Encircling the water was a bench whereby two middle-aged people, faces full of sorrow, sat hand in hand. It was at their feet where Christopher and his trustworthy companions gently landed, all thanks to the gracious wings of the honeybees.

"Greetingzzz, Blind King and Deaf Queen," Blossom addressed the monarchs cordially, bowing in respect.

The travelers marveled at the royal couple who were arrayed in purple robes, fitted with white silk slippers, and heads crowned with coronets of gold. Abounding with devotion for one another, the king communicated to his wife by making finger movements in her hands while she in turn whispered into her husband's ear.

"Greetings to you, Blossom," the king responded solemnly, staring directly ahead and tenderly caressing the queen's hands.

"The Creator hazzz azzzked uzzz to bear thezzze zzzervantzzz of Hizzz to you," the honeybee motioned with her antennae. The party dismounted, bowed, and properly introduced themselves to the noble couple.

"Weee were not told youuu were blind and deaf," Nathanael slurred in embarrassment.

Exchanging gestures, the royal couple smiled warmly at the gentle giant.

"I respond graciously to his touch, he listens attentively to my words and together we converse in love," the queen responded, looking at her husband admiringly.

"Where are the zzzubjectzzz of your kingdom?" Blossom asked apprehensively.

The queen relayed the question to the king who answered while simultaneously providing an explanation for their sadness.

"They are home," he sighed deeply, his response filled with anguish, "mourning the death of their children."

27
Mourning at the Palace

*Therefore let those who suffer according to the will of God
commit their souls to Him in doing good, as to a faithful Creator.*
1 Peter 4:19

"Nimrod is to blame for this!" Samuel exclaimed in righteous anger.

"Yes," the Blind King admitted with displeasure, "and it is because our people have in faith held steadfast to the promise of everlasting life which comes from the Creator, through His Son, and in the power of the Holy Breeze. We have steadfastly refused allegiance to the Dark Emperor and he has in return bequeathed to us severe persecution, the worst of it coming three nights ago for it was then a raven flew overhead, cawing out a curse:

"Come out, come out, my pretty little limbless ones!
Come out, come out, and kiss their little helpless ones!"'

123

Christopher and his friends glanced at one another in disgust, recalling Nimrod's elation when mentioning judgment upon the people of the East Kingdom.

"The next day," the king continued, "serpents black as coal emerged from beneath the ground, from the Underworld, and entered every household throughout our land, biting every child and poisoning them with venom, robbing them of life."

"Now I know why the Daughters of Time urged me to quickly deliver the seed," Christopher spoke sullenly, "but it appears my arrival is too late."

"What seed do you speak of?" questioned the Deaf Queen with assistance from her husband.

The seed-bearer drew forth the wooden vessel and handed it to the queen. Unlatching the lid and gazing at its contents she took a deep breath and shared the findings with her husband whose face erupted into sheer astonishment. Christopher then proceeded with a brief discourse of who he was and from where he had traveled but in the midst of his narrative and quite suddenly the Holy Breeze swept down amongst the small congregation, whisking the seed out of its repository and casting it into the pool. The blood-covered gift of love dissolved, immediately brightening the water like lightning and making it clear as glass. A sweet aroma then filled the air and the Voice, beautiful and full of grace, beckoned...

"Oh, taste and see that the LORD is good;

Blessed in the man who trusts in Him!"

Christopher blushed at the all too familiar sound.

Comprehending fully the promise unfolding before them, the king proclaimed, "It is not too late! The Creator's timing is always perfect! Quick, gather the children to the fountain!"

28
The Gift...

He has delivered us from the power of darkness and conveyed us into the kingdom of the Son of His love, in Whom we have redemption through His blood, the forgiveness of sins.
Colossians 1:13-14

Before anyone could say the word *'honey'* Blossom buzzed and a swarm of bees quickly emerged overhead. Without any further explanation, Blossom and Bess along with their fellow pollen collectors led the way to every household in the kingdom and within moments returned, the droning of wings again filling the air.

"I wonder who that could *'bee'*?" Petra joshed whimsically.

Clinging tenaciously to the neck of each honeybee were fathers cradling their lifeless children. The regiment of gigantic insects alighted in the courtyard and the children were carried to the pool.

"Place the children in the water!" the Blind King bellowed.

With that decree every boy and girl was tenderly immersed into the pool where they miraculously resurrected to life!

"The water is not for the children only but for us too!" the Deaf Queen proclaimed excitedly.

"The Creator's desire is that we draw near to Him through the blood of His Son," Samuel added with adoration.

With the compassionate and reassuring Voice calling out to all, the small group knelt in humble repentance and thanksgiving at the pool's encircling bench.

"With faith, let us drink the covenant of promise," the king declared with gratitude.

Thirsty for new life each person drew forth the liquid to their lips and drank, savoring every drop. Only Christopher did not participate in the act of worship as both pride and shame arose within his heart, restraining him again from partaking of the gift.

"All praise to the Creator!" the Blind King shouted joyfully. "I am clean thanks to the blood of His Son!"

"Drinking this living water makes our hearts pure!" the Deaf Queen professed.

"Look!" Petra hollered, pointing towards the pool. "A glimpse of the assurance we have inherited everlasting life!"

Peering with wonder into the pool all were jubilant to see their glorified images visible on the water's surface: the Blind King was no longer blind, the Deaf Queen no longer deaf, Samuel was again a healthy young man, Petra's left shoulder was restored along with his body of green newly polished, and Nathanael no longer exhibited any deformities.

"The best is yet to come," the Blind King acknowledged, "for on the Day of our glorification we will then eat the fruit from the Tree of Life!"

It was then through the gates of the courtyard the mothers and other family members streamed, they also feasting on the water and roaring with hallelujahs to the Creator, His Son, and the Holy Breeze.

"I must return to the people in the North Kingdom and tell them they, too, can receive forgiveness and newness of life!" Samuel commented happily.

"Myyy peeeople in the South Kingdom must liiikewiiise drink the water sooo theeey too maaay knooow the truth!" Nathanael expressed with conviction.

"Let us not forget the people in the West Kingdom!" Petra rejoiced.

"Queen Bernizzze will mozzzt zzzertainly buzzzzzz with joy," Bess hummed to her fellow arthropods, "for today there izzz zzzomething much zzzweeter to drink than honey!"

"Let us celebrate the Creator's love with a great banquet!" the Blind King shouted enthusiastically.

In the midst of the exultant crowd, however, there was one individual who could not join in the festivities…the seed-bearer himself. Eyes blurred with tears, he gazed forlornly into the water that shimmered with the light of life. Convinced by pride he was undeserving, Christopher stubbornly turned away from the pool. It was at that foreordained moment in time, despite all hope seemingly lost, when the Creator's sovereignty in pursuing the boy was made manifest: as in the attic, the Holy Breeze mercifully, tenderly, and lovingly combed through his hair.

"No one deserves the water, Christopher. It is a gift received by faith alone," the Voice spoke lovingly.

In that moment and in his heart of hearts Christopher surrendered and knelt at the liquid altar. Cupping his hands he submerged them into the cool water, sparkling like a jewel in his palms.

"Forgive me of my selfishness," he petitioned with sincere humility. "Please, save me from myself."

Drawing the water to his mouth he closed his eyes and drank.

Immediately, the guilt, rebellion, selfishness, and shame that had tormented him was completely washed away! Peace and joy filled his spirit, body, and soul, instilling within his being an overwhelming desire to serve the Creator, His Son, and the Holy Breeze. His face burst forth with an uncontrollable smile, body giggling with happiness.

"The water is alive!" Christopher laughed aloud. "The water is truly alive!"

29
...and the Giver

Jesus said to him, "I am the way, the truth, and the life.
No one comes to the Father except through Me."
John 14:6

"*Yes, Christopher, the water is alive and now so are you,*" the Voice agreed delightfully from behind him.

Opening his eyes Christopher was relieved to see the image of his glorified state, a mature man both physically and in faith, dancing upon the water's surface. He was surprised to discover, however, he was no longer at the palace of the East Kingdom but rather once again at the Fountain of Living Waters on the Island of Time. Turning, he squint as incarnate deity beamed affectionately down upon him: eyes of flaming fire, brow and wrists scarred and stained with His very own blood; everlasting life is freely offered to all who will believe but it was procured at a great cost. Realizing no good work could ever warrant this love Christopher kneeled, worshipping the Creator's Son.

"Fulfilling the Creator's sovereign will, cleansed by My blood, and sustained by the power of the Holy Breeze, you have delivered Our gift of love to the Elect in the Land of the Four Kingdoms," He declared victoriously, radiating majestic splendor. *"Being one of the Elect, you were chosen to be the seed-bearer though your heart was also in need of purifying. Once returning to the world appointed you, drink daily from the water I have given your people, the Book of Life, as it will be a reminder of My promises for someday I will make all things new."*

The boy nodded remembering he had received a copy of the sacred manuscript from his parents this past Christmas.

"What about my friends, Natalie and Scott and-" Christopher began to question.

"A reunion with your friends is not now ordained. However, if your paths cross again in this life you must share with them My love."

Despite those disappointing words the boy was content, heart filled with peace beyond earthly understanding.

"Christopher," the Son spoke jubilantly, *"your ride home has arrived!"*

30
Homeward Bound

Fear not, for I am with you; Be not dismayed, for I am your God.
I will strengthen you, yes, I will help you,
I will uphold you with My righteous right hand.
Isaiah 41:10

"Cumulus!" Christopher cheered, face breaking into a grin.

With the appearance of his friend of white he realized the Creator's Son had vanished.

"Christopher!" the Cloud Man responded with exuberance. "My, how good it is to see you and cheerful at that! How have you been these past seven days?"

"Wonderful," the boy answered truthfully, "and I cannot wait to tell you all about it."

"I look forward to every word," Cumulus said, extending his hand enthusiastically.

Ascending, during the next few hours Christopher shared with Cumulus his adventures in the Land of the Four Kingdoms.

133

"Once drinking from the Fountain of Living Waters I became clean from the inside out," Christopher concluded.

"I have no doubt of that," Cumulus agreed, "for you are indeed a changed boy, a new person."

The sky turned from blue to orange and finally sable when the moon appeared, shining with delight from above.

"As promised," Cumulus began, recalling his pledge, "the Master of Time Himself has preserved and safely seen you home before dawn," and with those words they glided into the attic just as the grandfather clock downstairs began chiming four o'clock.

"I did not have the opportunity to say good-bye to Petra, Nathanael, Samuel, or my other new friends," Christopher sighed regretfully.

"Do not be dismayed," the Cloud Man encouraging him, "I am certain you will see them again but until then, I vow to pass on your love."

"Will I ever see *Him* again?" Christopher asked hopefully.

"Oh, yes, Christopher, you *will* see Him again," Cumulus spoke confidently, eyes twinkling, "for I myself will someday accompany Him when He returns, glorifying you and all those He dearly loves. Until That Day arrives, however, we must serve Him faithfully."

The boy removed his shoes and outer clothing, climbed into bed, and nestled between clean white sheets, resting his weary head upon the pillow.

"Good night, Christopher," came the peaceful words of the Cloud Man, his billowing form drifting out of the attic and into the night beyond.

"Good night, Cumulus," Christopher whispered dreamily, the hope of life everlasting comforting him until the light of a new day.

Made in the USA
Coppell, TX
17 April 2021

53991940R00079